Praise for Redemption Road

"In the tradition of Liberian literary greats Bai T. Moore and Wilton Sankawulo, Elma Shaw carves out a period in Liberia's history and transplants it onto paper for the world to swallow and digest without judgment. *Redemption Road* reminds us of our tragic past but it also shows us that peace, justice, reconciliation, progress, and development are attained if we only try a little harder."
— from the Foreword by Ellen Johnson Sirleaf,
President, Republic of Liberia

"The choices that Bendu makes teach lessons in much the way that Chinua Achebe aims at educating his African readers. Shaw has taken an enormously difficult theme and treated it convincingly after laying the horrific groundwork of what happens during time of awful warfare—especially to women. Atonement and renewal as Shaw develops them are believable and inspiring and exactly what so many potential readers in Africa need during these troubled times. I see *Redemption Road* finding many enthusiastic readers not only in Liberia, but also in Sierra Leone, South Africa, Rwanda, Congo—a list that sadly can be expanded too far."
— Charles R. Larson, *Department of Literature,*
American University

"Elma Shaw swims through the murky depths of Liberia's recent past without holding her breath. She breathes and allows us to breathe through the pain. Her *Redemption Road* is a story that needs to be told and Shaw handles the emotions, the tragedy, the wounds, and the burden, with delicacy and power."
— Stephanie Horton, *Sea Breeze Journal*
of Contemporary Liberian Writings

"Liberia could very well enter the canon of post-conflict literature with Elma Shaw's *Redemption Road*. Peppered with flashbacks, chock full of suspense, and sprinkled with a smidgen of romance, *Redemption Road* contextualizes the Liberian Civil War with gut-wrenching appeal...It brings to bear Liberia's tortured history, and civil conflict no doubt, but it also transcends the country's context to ask universal questions about truth, reconciliation, forgiveness, and the power of unconditional love."

— Robtel Neajai Pailey, *LIBERIA Travel & Life Magazine*

"A brilliant novel...a promising and incisive voice. Elma Shaw knows how to tell a story. Reading *Redemption Road* was a most refreshing and enlightening experience, and the best Liberian novel I have ever read. It will go a long way in placing Liberia on the map of world literature."

— Wilton Sankawulo, *Professor of English and Literature, University of Liberia,* and author of *Sundown at Dawn*

"Elma Shaw's novel is a journey back to the ruins of our homeland, where the beauty of culture clashes with the ugliness of war. It is a story filled with both life and death, but throughout *Redemption Road,* I feel the power of hope in both the storyteller and the novel's heroine."

— Patricia Jabbeh Wesley, author of *Becoming Ebony* and *The River is Rising*

"...spellbinding...*Redemption Road* holds your attention without end. If you survived a war or lost loved ones in a war, you will relate to this tear-jerking story of fear, survival, life, power and love. I highly recommend this page-turner."

— Angela M. Peabody, author of *Exiled – within the heart of American society*

Redemption Road

Redemption Road

The Quest for Peace and Justice in Liberia

Elma Shaw

cottonTree
P r e s s

REDEMPTION ROAD
Copyright © 2008 by Elma Shaw

First Cotton Tree Press hardcover edition: August 2008

Published by Cotton Tree Press
Washington DC
Monrovia, Liberia
www.CottonTreePress.com

Library of Congress Control Number: 2007908088

ISBN 978-0-9800774-0-7 (Trade Hardcover)
ISBN 978-0-9800774-1-4 (Trade Paperback)

Printed in the United States of America

About the cover photograph:
On April 12, 1980, a group of 17 noncommissioned officers from the Armed Forces of Liberia walked a path along the ocean behind their barracks, and up to the Executive Mansion at the top of the hill. There, they assassinated President William R. Tolbert, Jr. Ten days later, their new government—the People's Redemption Council—executed 13 high-ranking officials of Tolbert's government on the beach by the same path they had taken. The path was soon transformed, and they officially named it "Redemption Road".

6°18' 15. 74" N   10°48' 14. 08" W

*In memory of Famatta Sherman Nah
and Nabile Hage*

*for all those who died
for all those still missing
and for all of us still alive*

and

*In memory of my grandmothers
Eugenia Cooper Shaw and Joetta Greaves
who were such influential
and loving matriarchs*

Foreword

In the tradition of Liberian literary greats Bai T. Moore and Wilton Sankawulo, Elma Shaw carves out a period in Liberia's history and transplants it onto paper for the world to swallow and digest without judgment. *Redemption Road* reminds us of our tragic past but it also shows us that peace, justice, reconciliation, progress, and development are attained if we only try a little harder.

There comes a time in every country's history when things go astray, when we don't put our best faces forward, when we falter and stumble. Liberia faltered and stumbled time and time again for over a century. Now we're taking bold steps to walk upright again, holding our heads up high. *Redemption Road* reminds us of those times of knee deep failure, and yet, it also shows us that Liberia will rise again through the potential of our most prized possession—our will as a people to transcend.

This book has the potential to reach deep into the soul of every Liberian. *Redemption Road* strikes a special chord with me because the protagonist, Bendu Lewis, is a woman who must confront her past, and the memories attached to that past. It is about accepting our vices as human, forgiving ourselves, and allowing others to heal.

The tragedy of war reveals the potential for humans to behave with ruthless disregard for life, but it also allows people to reconnect with their own humanity. The Liberian Civil War was tragic, yes, but there are countless examples of families taking in orphans, combatants shielding potential victims, strangers embracing strangers. This attests to the

Liberian spirit of forgiveness and reconciliation, of communalism and commonality. *Redemption Road* fictionalizes a historical moment, and it also puts a human face to the war's wrath. It reminds us that ultimately, Liberians must take ownership of the past, reconcile with the present, and plan for a better future.

I commend Ms. Shaw for taking a bold step in what can only be described as a valiant attempt to recount unspeakable truths about Liberia's history, leaving us with hope that the future is still ours to capture and change. I hope that the publication of this novel will encourage more Liberians to write and publish because words create documentation. We have a rich literary history that must continue and thrive for generations to come. *Redemption Road* catapults us back on that turning wheel.

Ellen Johnson Sirleaf
President, Republic of Liberia

re · demp · tion (noun)
1 the action of saving or being saved from sin, error or evil.
2 the action of regaining or gaining possession of something in exchange for payment, or clearing a debt. (Oxford American Dictionaries)

1980: Redemption is here
One mother rejoices
One mother grieves
One woman dances
One woman weeps

And what, pray tell
Was Redemption Road paved with?
Good intentions
Aid from abroad
Greed
Blood
Rigged elections
More blood
And still, more aid

So, 1990: Redemption comes again
This time almost everyone rejoices
Then everyone grieves
Almost everyone dances
Then everyone weeps

Over a decade of turmoil
And prayers for Peace

Part One

Time Heals Nothing

Chapter 1

As people paid their last respects to Catherine May Tyler Lewis, they were either reverently silent, or they broke down and cried. Some reached to the heavens and, oblivious to everyone around them, talked to Catherine loudly. For Bendu Lewis, Catherine's granddaughter, the pain was magnified for she was the last to see Granny May alive. It was she who had watched her die an undignified death, emaciated legs and arms dangling over the side of a dirty, rusty wheelbarrow.

Hundreds of friends and relatives had come now to celebrate the old lady's life and mourn her death. Their emotions were raw and intense, even though she had died almost ten years earlier. Although the remains of Catherine Lewis had never been found, the family had decided to use a casket anyway, and had placed in it a large portrait of their matriarch along with a few things that reflected what she loved most: her Bible, a collage of family pictures, a framed picture of her husband Samuel Lewis II (who had died long before the war), a single white rose, and the red white and blue flag of Liberia.

Bendu watched her father, Benjamin Lewis, move steadily among the crowd, comforting friends and relatives with words here, a touch there, a reassuring smile, or a story to remind them of his mother's generosity and sense of humor. Bendu's mother Eva was there too, sitting with old Cousin Rebecca, and they were glancing over at Bendu every now and then with what seemed like disapproval in their eyes.

Ben and Eva Lewis left Liberia in the early 1990s, not long after Charles Taylor escaped from an American prison and entered Liberia on a mission to unseat President Samuel K. Doe. Now, after nine years of factional fighting, and mission long ago accomplished, Taylor was President of Liberia. Disgusted with the election that gave him power, Ben and Eva had only returned from the States for the memorial service. All their property had been destroyed during the civil war, and they were staying with Siatta, Bendu's older sister, and her husband Terrance Clarke. Siatta had left the US and returned to Terrance a few months before the memorial. Despite sporadic rebel attacks, she had decided to stay in Liberia for good now that Terrance was part of the elected government and there was relative peace.

Ben and Eva had no plans to stay for good. Undone first by the 1980 *coup d'état* in which they lost political power and their only son, then the civil war a decade later, they felt Liberia now was just too different from the one they had enjoyed. They were unwilling to aid the country's development and often joked that their daughter Bendu was their great contribution.

None of them will ever understand my pain, Bendu thought, looking around and fanning herself for relief from the heat that would only be mitigated by the next rainfall. She slowly tuned out what the people around her were saying and fixed her eyes on the shiny, satin-lined casket at the other end of the room. Then she heard the voice:

"You girl, leave that old woman and run!"

Oh, the voices! Bendu could not forget the voices mingled with screams as the whole population of Charlue Town and surrounding villages ran for their lives. People at the memorial service swirled around her in a hazy sea of black, purple and white—the standard mourning colors—and their sounds soon meshed with the sounds in her head.

That day, as they ran, with Bendu pushing her sick grand-mother in a wheelbarrow, a matronly woman grabbed her by the shoulders and shook her. "Old Ma's time is finished! She's old, you are young. Come let's go!"

The sound of the machine guns was getting louder and they heard screaming in the distance behind them. The screams were almost drowned out though, by the piercing wails of several abandoned babies and small children by the roadside. Their parents or guardians were either unable or unwilling to carry them any further, or had simply lost them in the confusion. A few of the children ran scared among the crowd, stretching out their arms and crying, in vain, to be picked up. They ran, but their little legs couldn't get them far, and Bendu gasped in horror as she saw a couple of them trampled by the frightened adults. She would remember the terror on their little faces forever. She wanted to gather up some of the babies and put them in the wheelbarrow with Granny May, but she knew that would only slow them down.

All around, Bendu saw that several elderly and sick people had also been left behind. A few struggled to follow the crowd. Others made no attempt and sat crying, praying, calling out to the able-bodied running past them: "Ay my daughter! Ay my son! Help me o, help me, I beg you!" Still others sat silently, and stared blankly as they awaited their fate.

Bendu gripped the wheelbarrow handles more firmly, and pushed ahead. Granny May had withered to about 90 pounds, but Bendu had lost weight herself, and strength too, so it was not easy. Her jeans sagged on her a bit and she wished she had worn a *lappa* instead. The large piece of fabric would have been a better fit wrapped tightly around her waist, and would have helped her blend in with the other, more traditionally dressed women. She could also have used it as a blanket for Granny May or as a head-tie to wrap up her own conspicuously long hair. It was so important not to stand out among the crowd. Anything remarkable made it too easy to be pulled out of crowds at the checkpoints that were being set up along the major roads. She thanked God now that she was dark-skinned; her complexion helped her blend in with the people around her.

Suddenly, a shrill whistling sound pierced the sky behind the fleeing crowd. For a few seconds, they slowed down as they tried to figure out what invisible aircraft was flying their way. The whistling stopped abruptly and the gigantic explosion that followed stunned them. A rocket-propelled grenade had landed in the village they had just abandoned.

Dizzy. Slow motion. Confusion. Then utter bedlam as people regained their hearing and began to run even faster.

Bendu, too, panicked and found some energy to run for a bit.

One more person shouted at her as he ran past. "Leave that wheelbarrow, you girl! Your Old Ma's looking dead already. Just leave her!"

But Bendu ran and pushed until two of the painful blisters in her hands burst and her weary legs crumpled beneath her. She fell to her knees, panting, out of breath, a sharp stabbing pain in her right side. She rested her head on the wheelbarrow and tried to catch her breath as the last of the villagers rushed by.

"Granny May? Don't worry Granny May. We *will* get out of here together. I promise you," she assured the old woman.

With the crowd and their noise now gone ahead, Bendu finally heard her grandmother's hoarse whisper. "Leave me baby. Go. Save yourself."

Bendu scooped her grandmother up tenderly and held her in her arms. "No Granny May, no! I'll never leave you!" Granny May's skin was hot and dry, and she smelled of the Vicks ointment that she rubbed on her chest to ward off coughs and colds.

Granny May whispered again, this time more faintly. "Go baby. My Lord will take care of me. He will take care of you too." With those words her body went limp and Bendu stumbled as she placed her grandmother back in the wheelbarrow. Granny May's thin eyelids closed and a rasping sound came out of her throat.

"Granny May?"

The old woman was silent and still.

"Granny May?" Bendu shook her gently.

A thin old man rose up from the grass on the roadside and limped over to look at them. "*Nama*, fine girl," he said. "Sorry yah? You did well to stay with your Ma. God will bless you."

Bendu stared at the old man for a few seconds, then shook her head slowly as she began to understand what he was saying. She stumbled backward, eyes still on him, searching his wrinkled face.

"No," she whispered. "No!"

The man simply lowered his head sadly before he turned and walked away.

Bendu scrambled to her feet, pushed the wheelbarrow to the side of the road, collapsed beside it and wept bitterly until her eyes were swollen and her jaws hurt. She was crying so hard she didn't see the fighters until they were standing right in front of her. The leaders wore army fatigues and berets. Most of the others with them were a ragtag bunch, but all of them had weapons and some of the men were wearing wigs. They were obviously not from the Armed Forces of Liberia. There were about thirty people in all, including a few very young boys and several women. To everyone's great surprise, Bendu looked right at them and sucked her teeth loudly. A man with wild dreadlocks stepped forward with a scowl on his face, raised the handle of his gun, and was about to bring it down full force on her head when his commander grabbed his arm and stopped him. Bendu hadn't even flinched. She didn't care anymore. She was tired of the war, tired of running, and wanted to die herself, right there with Granny May. She wished someone would just shoot her and end the pain. A bullet would send her to heaven where she would get to see her beloved fiancé Jonah once more.

The commander was a tall muscular man with a moustache and '70s style sideburns.

"Stand up!" he ordered in the dialect that most people in the region spoke.

Bendu rose to her feet slowly. Her legs and arms were sore from pushing Granny May in the wheelbarrow for miles.

Still speaking in the dialect, the man in charge introduced himself. "I am Commander Cobra. Who are you?" he asked.

"My name is Bendu," she replied.

"Bendu what?"

"Bendu Lewis."

Murmurs in the crowd. "She's a *Congo* girl," someone said. "Listen to her voice; she's Americo-Liberian."

"How come you know my dialect?" the commander asked.

Bendu decided not to say that her fiancé spoke it and taught her a little before he died. "I took classes at the University of Liberia."

Commander Cobra nodded, obviously impressed. "You speak it well."

"She sucked her teeth at us!" the angry man with the gun interrupted. "Let me strike for you Cobra!"

"Don't worry Samson," the commander said, eyes still on Bendu, and speaking English now. "I will strike for myself."

Samson stepped back and grinned at the thought.

"What were you doing in Charlue Town?" the commander asked Bendu.

"My grandmother and I were visiting relatives in Sumoville when the big bridge was destroyed. We couldn't get back to Monrovia."

One of the boys looked over at the old woman in the wheelbarrow and asked "Your Old Ma's sleeping or what?" The woman standing next to him sucked her teeth and knocked him on the head with the back of her hand. "The Old Ma's dead and you're asking if she's sleeping?" A few of the fighters snickered.

"So, where are you carrying the body?" the commander asked Bendu. His question drew more laughter. Bendu choked on her pain and couldn't answer.

"Fall in line. You're coming with us," he ordered.

Bendu stepped behind the wheelbarrow and picked up the handles with her bloody hands. It seemed like everyone started shouting and laughing at her at once:

"Where are you carrying that dead body?"

"No morgue where we going, o!"

"Put that damn wheelbarrow down!"

"Look at all these bodies lying around. This is your Old Ma's graveyard right here!"

Bendu collapsed on top of her grandmother and let out an anguished cry. Two men grabbed her and tried to pull her off but she gripped the sides of the wheelbarrow and would not let go.

"I'm staying here!" she screamed. "I don't care what you say, I'm staying here!" The commander turned away from Bendu, motioned to some of the men, and led them forward along the road. He turned back to Samson and the others, and, tossing his head in Bendu's direction, ordered them to put an end to the nonsense and bring her quickly.

One of the young women moved forward to try and console the distressed girl, but before she could say anything Samson raised his gun again and brought it down hard on Bendu's fingers with a sickening crack. She let go of the wheelbarrow and the men were able to drag her away screaming in agony. She soon fell unconscious from the pain, the hunger, the shock of what had happened to Granny May, and of what was happening to her.

When she finally woke up, it was dark and the fighters were quietly setting up camp in the woods.

Someone put a comforting hand on her shoulder, and Bendu was startled out of her thoughts. She blinked and looked around her now, at her family and at the friends who had come to Granny May's memorial service to sympathise with her. There was Agnes, a colleague from the peace education center; several of their students—including Tenneh, who had been hospitalized with malaria all week and was supposed to still be in bed recovering; and Calvin Daniels, a childhood friend. Bendu was grateful for their presence, but in a way, she just wanted to be left alone. Although they did give her some sort of support, the fact that she could never tell them everything actually made her grief more unbearable, the pain more intense. What if they found out what had happened to her, or what she had done? Would they understand? Would her family forgive her? Sometimes it all seemed so far away, the nightmare that was the war. But sometimes the memories were so sharp they left her debilitated. A year with the fighters had changed her life forever, and she couldn't understand how so many war survivors could say so easily "forget it, let it go," or "let bygones be bygones." For Bendu, forgetting was out of the question, but remembering and doing nothing about it was even worse.

Chapter 2

$\sim$

As the driver parked the Pajero at the Temple of Justice, Moses Varney looked at the bumper sticker pasted on the dashboard: IN THE CAUSE OF THE PEOPLE, THE STRUGGLE CONTINUES. It was the rallying cry of President Doe and his People's Redemption Council in the days following the 1980 coup, but Varney had not yet stopped using it. He got out of the passenger seat of the large vehicle and strode quickly toward the courthouse. There wasn't much time to lose; too many lives were hanging in the balance. *Why am I always in charge when lives are hanging in the balance?* he wondered. Varney's driver, who also served as his bodyguard, followed close behind him. But Varney wasn't fast enough to escape the attention of the small group of teenage boys hanging out near the courthouse parking lot perched up on the Capitol Bypass.

"Brother V! Brother V!" they called, as they rushed toward him.

Varney muttered something under his breath and slowed down to acknowledge them with a wave of his hand.

The bodyguard, a dark wiry man known to everyone simply as Weah, turned to face the boys and half-heartedly tried to drive them away.

"That's okay Weah," Varney said, stepping up behind him. "These are my boys."

Weah stepped aside and the boys grinned and slapped palms with their friend. One of them berated the bodyguard. "That's our *poppay* here. You can't stop us from talking to him."

"No way!" another boy said. "It's true—he's our father."

Varney smiled. The boy who had spoken up first was called Simeon. Varney also knew Alphonso, the smallest one. He recognized some of the others but didn't remember their names. They had grown up so fast. The boys looked up at him now, expectantly.

"We're still here o," Simeon said, the pep gone from his voice.

Varney swallowed hard and placed a heavy hand on Simeon's shoulder. "I see you," he said solemnly, knowing that was not enough. Varney knew all too well what it was like to be young, displaced and unemployed. When he was just 11 years old, he was with his parents in a crowded minibus traveling from Sanniquellie to Monrovia, when the driver lost control and tumbled into a ravine. The bus was made to hold 15 passengers, but the owner had restructured the inside to take almost twice the limit. The roof of the bus was piled high with bags, market produce, several chickens, a goat, and a small pig. Ten people lost their lives that day, including his parents. After the accident, his two younger sisters were taken in by his mother's sister, and he was sent to Monrovia to live with his uncle. It was not a time he liked to think about, but it was a time that changed the course of his life.

Varney focused on Simeon's face. He could see the boy had not yet lost hope, despite all he had lived through. But what would his future be like? And would Alphonso too have to grow up on the street? Time was not waiting, but by the Grace of God, he vowed silently, things were going to change.

"I won't forget you," Varney promised the boys before he walked away. He looked toward the Temple of Justice looming in the distance and thought of the men who sat in those seats for so many years only to be "surprised" by how bad the system was when it was their turn to face it. Justice. Where was the justice in this godforsaken place? In *his* day they used to call for justice. Nowadays everyone was calling for peace. When would they understand? There can never be true peace in Liberia until there's equity for the masses. *No justice, no peace.* How many times did they have to say it? He only wished the people would rise up to liberate themselves. That was key. The task was daunting, but not impossible. He remembered the days, long past, when they tried to teach the people about their rights. How he would hold up a textbook and tell them it was their weapon of liberation. It wasn't easy, when sometimes over half of the group could not read or write. Still, he had believed in the dream with all his heart.

Varney entered the Temple of Justice and made his way to the Judiciary wing. He stopped in front of a large ornate door and weighed his choices for what seemed like the millionth time. Then he took a deep breath and knocked on the door with a renewed determination. *In the cause of the people, the struggle has continued long enough,* he thought. *Now it's time for the struggle to end.*

Chapter 3

Bendu got out of the crowded yellow taxi at Broad and Mechlin Streets and handed the driver a 10 Liberian Dollar note. She was thankful that despite the worry caused by rebel incursions and UN-imposed sanctions on the country, the exchange rate was holding steady at 50 LD to one US dollar. She was also glad to be going back to work after taking time off for her grandmother's memorial service, but the smell of the raw sewage that had overflowed into the street with the torrential August rain ruined the joy of the short hike up the hill. The scent was nothing though, Bendu had to admit, compared to the stench of the rotting bodies that littered this very intersection when she returned from behind the lines a few years ago. Broad Street was once more a lively, bustling hub of informal sector activity mingled with large banks, office buildings, government ministries, stationery stores, and now, internet cafés. The large, flamboyant trees which grew in the center median—all the way from Snapper Hill to Crown Hill—were full of their pretty orange-red blossoms and provided canopies of shade and carpets of flowers and roots. Nothing could take away her love for Monrovia, the coastal capital where she was born and raised. But still, sometimes Bendu couldn't help remembering the mess she had seen when she returned: the telephone wires and cables destroyed and hanging down into the street; the bullet-riddled buildings; the bodies of men, women and children in various stages of decay. Broad Street was a frightful sight, and if anyone had told her then that someday she'd be running a local Non-Governmental Organization right in the center of where that chaos was, she would not have believed it.

Bendu finally arrived at a freshly whitewashed building and made her way upstairs to the Peace in Practice office. The reception area of the NGO was decorated with poster-sized photographs of PIP in action: helping disarm child soldiers, showing off arts and crafts made in the vocational training classes, conducting HIV and AIDS awareness and prevention programs, and, her favorite: walking with their banner held high during the 2001 Women's March for Peace. Bendu paused in front of the photograph, as she always did. It was a daily ritual that reminded her of her *raison d'être*—her reason for waking up each morning and putting her heart and soul into the work that she did. That sunny May day during the peace march, when they stopped at the American Embassy to read their Resolutions, women started crying spontaneously. One by one—young women, old women, the well-educated, and the unlettered. But it was not the loud wailing of women in despair. It was not bitter, and it was not angry. It was as quiet as if they had the weight of their losses pressing down around their hearts and throats. The weeping spread like wildfire as they expressed the collective pain that had gathered in the depths of their souls. They wept for their lost babies, their lost futures, and their lost dignity. It was a haunting echo of past laments and a plea for the situation at hand. It had been four years since Taylor was elected, and new rebels had been fighting government forces and terrorizing citizens in Lofa County and other places for the last two of those years now. Everyone feared that without international action, the violence would soon reach Monrovia. *No more,* the women begged that day. *Please, stop this war!*

Bendu took a deep breath and glanced at the clock on the wall. It told her she had exactly fifteen minutes before her 10 o'clock appointment.

Agnes Jallah, PIP's co-director, was already at work arranging chairs for a group counseling session. She was Bendu's age, but had not had much formal education beyond high school. Bendu had selected her as a partner though, because of Agnes' passion and for the way she could reach the clients PIP was designed to help. Agnes was reluctant to be given the title and responsibility of co-director, but Bendu had insisted.

The women greeted each other warmly, and Agnes smiled, showing the wide gap between her two front teeth. "Calvin came to see you this morning," she said.

"What did he want?"

"I don't know, but if it had something to do with the center he would have talked to me, not so? Maybe he was looking for *you,* Bendu." Agnes smiled and winked.

Bendu laughed. Her friend Calvin had visited her at the center once or twice and had co-sponsored one of their events. Agnes had been trying to play matchmaker ever since she met him. It was a hopeless effort though, and Calvin seemed to have no time to listen to Agnes' hints and pleas.

"Calvin's considering giving us some real money," Bendu said as she headed to her office, "but if he's looking for something else first, he'd better go find it in a different place."

Agnes followed her and stood at the door while Bendu poured herself some hot water from the flask.

Bendu looked around at her and shook her head. "You don't give up, do you?"

"Give him a chance," Agnes urged. "He's a very nice man. And *fine*, too! What are you so scared of?"

Bendu didn't answer. She agreed. Calvin *was* nice and handsome. But there was so much more to consider.

"Look, you girl," Agnes said gently, "you can't let your past rule your future."

Bendu sat down at her desk with her cup of tea. "Wait. Isn't that what we're supposed to do? Learn from the past?"

Agnes sighed. "Of course, but remember, you didn't make a mistake. What happened to Jonah was the will of God. When the food in your pot is finished you will never eat again?"

Bendu laughed despite herself, and Agnes grinned. "Think about it," she said with a wink. And with that, she left Bendu alone and went back to her own office.

Bendu sighed and sipped her tea. *Ah, the Jonah past. Is that what I'm doing? Letting an unfortunate incident of fate scare me away from love?* Bendu put the cup down and rubbed her temples. What happened to Jonah was more than unfortunate. Losing her first love had been like dying herself—all life, all heart and soul and joy ripped out of her body and thrown into the depths of the Atlantic. Jonah had been nothing like his Biblical namesake who tried to avoid his duty to God's people and ended up in the belly of a whale. Instead of just spewing forth rhetoric among friends like so many pseudo activists, he often gave rousing public lectures and led demonstrations to bring awareness to the injustices that permeated both rural and urban Liberian society. Bendu was awakened and motivated by his passion and his fearlessness. He was exactly what she wanted, and she knew it the day she met him. Granny May and Old Man Sam Lewis embraced and loved Jonah as a son. Not everyone approved of their relationship though. When they announced their engagement, her mother kept insisting she was too young. Bendu's father accepted her choice without a fuss, but also without the same enthusiasm he had shown for his politician son-in-law Terrance Clarke. Some people thought it happened too fast, and many others wondered silently—and a few aloud—why she didn't find a nice boy whose ancestors had come over to Liberia on a ship.

Bendu and Jonah never had a chance to show the world that they could make it; he died of an unknown cause just two months before the wedding. Bendu picked up the framed photo of them at their engagement party and looked at it wistfully. Their bodies were facing each other and they were holding hands. They had been looking into each other's eyes, but just before the photographer snapped the photo, Jonah had turned and smiled into the camera. As she always did, Bendu looked for some sort of sign that the end was near for him. Was there something in his eyes? In his smile? In his posture? No, there was nothing out of the ordinary. No telling aura picked up by the camera's sometimes magical lens. What she thought she *could* see was a soul brimming over with love for her. That was all. She put the photo back on her desk next to the crystal Madonna and Child paperweight that always prompted people to ask her if she was Catholic. Her thoughts drifted to Calvin. He had been her brother's best friend and was a witness to his murder in 1980. Calvin had never quite gotten over Benji's death. In fact, he had never quite gotten over the whole coup. What would they be like together, she and Calvin with their issues?

Bendu shook her head as if to clear it, and began putting together a packet of brochures, news clippings, and press releases about PIP's work. At precisely 10 am, there was a knock on her door. "Come in!" she called cheerfully.

When the door opened, her eyes widened in surprise to see Calvin standing there. He was a tall man with salt and pepper hair and dark eyes that twinkled when he smiled at her.

"Oh," Bendu said. "I was expecting someone else."

Calvin contorted his face into a pained expression.

"Calvin, really," she laughed. "I have an interview right now. Can we talk later?"

"No ma'am," he said as he approached her desk. He leaned over and kissed her on both cheeks, then grinned and handed her a business card. "Calvin J. Daniels. *World Journal.* I called, but your landline wasn't working so I came by earlier this morning to tell you in person."

Bendu looked at the card. "*You're* the writer who's going to interview me?" She looked up and smiled at him. "Congratulations! Since when?"

"Last Friday. I got a freelance contract with *World Journal.* I'll be covering the Mano River Union for them: Liberia, Guinea and Sierra Leone. Mostly political stories."

"And the occasional little NGO?"

"I practically begged for this assignment," Calvin said, glancing at her as he sat down to set up his tape recorder. "Not all my subjects are going to be as beautiful as you are."

Bendu smiled. "What about conflict of interest?"

"Oh, there's no 'conflict' here, believe me. I'm just interested. *Very* interested."

Bendu lowered her eyes, suddenly shy, and felt a warmth rush to her cheeks. "You know that's not what I meant," she said with a smile. "I'm talking about the fact that you're my friend *and* a donor to this center. One of our favorites, in fact."

Calvin smiled and raised his eyebrows. "Is that right?"

"Yes, but don't let that go to your head," Bendu replied. "Seriously, though, how can you write a fair and balanced story?"

"I know you people do good work, but don't worry—if I ever find some dirt I won't hesitate to report it."

Bendu laughed again. She could see why Agnes was charmed. She was also glad that the center would be featured in such a reputable magazine. Some of the local newspapers were so full of errors that their stories were virtually useless. Calvin was one of the best writers around, and *World Journal* was definitely top of the line. In fact, this article could prove to be a crucial step in the survival of the center. They were running out of their initial funding, and excellent press could help encourage more individuals and organizations to support their work.

The two friends talked at length. As the interview began to wind down, Calvin asked about the difficulties of the program. Bendu stopped to think for a moment. "One obstacle we face with every group—at least in the beginning—is a wall of silence," she answered. "It's difficult getting some women to open up and talk about what happened to them. It's just not in the African culture to bare our souls in public. So, when someone is too deeply hurt we don't push too hard, we just let her benefit from the stories of those who are able to share."

"And that's enough? It works?" Calvin asked.

"Sure. It doesn't always take full disclosure to be able to move on. Sometimes the quiet ones have the greatest influence in their communities when it comes to reconciliation and peace-building."

"Then why make anyone disclose anything at all?"

Bendu shrugged. "It's easier, I guess, when they can let the pain surface and let people challenge them to deal with it quickly and completely."

Calvin paused and leaned forward slightly. "And what's *your* story, Bendu?" he asked softly.

"What?"

"Your story. You've never told me. You've been talking about what happened to everyone else, but you lived here during the war too."

Bendu shifted in her seat and began to arrange the papers on her desk. "Well, yes, but this interview is not about me."

"Okay. Maybe you can tell me this," Calvin said. "For the story. How did you become involved in this work, and how has it changed you?"

"Oh, I just wanted to help war-affected women, that's all." Bendu handed him the press packet she had prepared. "For background info," she said.

"Thanks. But you didn't answer me. How has working with these women changed you?"

Bendu's stomach tightened with a familiar feeling of sickness and anxiety as she struggled mentally to remove herself from among the women he was talking about. She looked up and saw Calvin looking at her, waiting.

"They've changed me in so many ways," she said, repeating the spiel she gave whenever she talked privately to the center's visitors. "They're strong. Resilient. Unwavering in their faith, no matter what happens to them. I learn from them every day."

Calvin did not look impressed or surprised. He cocked his head as if to say 'Come on, I'm waiting for more.'

Bendu stood up. "Hey, we've been talking for quite a while, and I need to —"

"You're right," Calvin interrupted as he turned off his tape recorder. "I've actually run into my next appointment. It's been good talking to you." He stood up and looked a bit surprised when she reached out to shake his hand.

"Goodbye Calvin. I look forward to reading your article."

Calvin held her hand a little longer than necessary. "May I come by if I need anything else?"

"You'll be able to call," Bendu replied, relaxing again as she walked him to the door. "We're giving up on landlines and getting hooked up with LoneStar tomorrow. I'll call you with the number. We'll have a cell phone for Agnes too."

"Good! And may I call you for a date?"

"Calvin!"

He smiled. "Conflict of interest?"

"Big time!" she replied as she gave him a playful push out the door.

Bendu leaned against her closed door and sighed. She decided she would go catch the end of the group counseling session because she knew if she sat down at her desk, alone, she would start thinking about her "story." About the things Calvin wanted to dredge up. But those things were at the bottom of her soul and that's where she wanted them to stay for now.

Chapter 4

Bendu headed toward the one spacious room that they used for everything at the peace education center. Rosetta, Josephine, and Tenneh: These were the young women who would be in the counseling session today. Rosetta was a tough one. She was very bitter about losing her husband to ethnic violence during the war, negative about everything, and quick to stereotype everyone. Josephine was a big, friendly woman—a motherly figure who often helped the counselors by being open and honest and encouraging the younger women to follow suit. Tenneh was new. She worked as the cook's helper at Siatta's house, and Siatta had been complaining about her left and right. Bendu had recognized the symptoms immediately, and urged Siatta to send the girl to PIP twice a week. Siatta had fired her first, but at least she was here now, getting the help she needed. Like almost everyone in the country, the three girls had suffered terribly during the war and were trying to deal with various symptoms of post-traumatic stress. Tenneh wasn't lazy or irresponsible, as Siatta had said; it was her bouts with depression that sometimes kept her in bed for days at a time. At 22, she was the youngest among them and was still in high school, having lost several years due to the civil war. She was soft-spoken and kind, and when she was not depressed she was the most positive and fun-loving person around. After several weeks of individual and group counseling, the girls had finally begun to open up and some breakthroughs were on the horizon.

Bendu walked into the room and the group greeted her warmly, but quietly, as she joined the semi-circle. Their last assignment had been to write a letter to the person who had caused them the greatest pain during the war, and from past experience, this was usually a major turning point in the center's trauma therapy.

Tenneh stood up and faced them now, with her letter in her hand. She stood silent for a long while, staring at the words she had written on the page. Finally, she began to read with an expressive voice that trembled with emotion:

Dear Mama,

Sometimes I wonder if it was a dream, but I have the constant pain in my womb that tells me no, it was real. It really happened. My own mother betrayed me. You stood there that morning Mama, with a borrowed baby on your back, and you let those fighters take me away to save yourself and your precious boy-child. "No, take this one," you said, pushing me to them and grabbing Junior back. "This boy is too small to fight, but my daughter can cook. She can work. Me, I've still got a baby sucking titty. What good can I do for you?"

> *I was scared Mama. I didn't want to leave you*
> *and go with those men and their guns. But when I*
> *started crying and hanging on to you, you slapped*
> *me and pushed me again, right into their arms. "I*
> *beg you, take her. She's a girl; she can do anything,"*
> *you said. "Anything you want her to do."*

At this point Tenneh had to pause. Rosetta and Josephine, who were sitting on either side of her, reached out to comfort their friend. Tenneh looked at the ceiling and blinked rapidly, regained her composure, and with great effort and determination, continued:

> *After they had finished with me, I escaped and*
> *ran all the way back to you, Mama. Naked and*
> *bleeding and crying, expecting you to take me into*
> *your arms and comfort me. And instead you drove*
> *me away from the yard shouting, as if you didn't*
> *even know me: "Carry your naked self from here*
> *before the children see you!" Carry myself where?*
> *I was twelve Mama! Twelve years old! I didn't*
> *understand what had happened to me and I didn't*
> *know where to go. You drove me away Mama,*
> *and a stranger was the one who found a lappa*
> *that evening and wrapped it around me. It was a*
> *stranger who washed me and held me in her arms*
> *and said "nama baby, don't cry." You betrayed me*
> *Mama. You who I expected to protect me. You were*
> *the one who gave me away.*
>
> *Your own daughter,*
>
> *Tenneh*

Tenneh sat down, placed her chin in her hand and stared into space, sniffling and wiping her face with the small towel she carried everywhere.

Bendu clenched her jaws and flashed back to herself at twelve. Would she have survived such trauma? Such betrayal? Calvin and her brother Benji were both twelve at the time of the coup. She was only eight and very sheltered. Suddenly her heart skipped a beat. *What exactly had Calvin seen that April afternoon?*

Bendu breathed deeply and watched Agnes pace. She and Agnes had conducted many workshops and sessions since they started Peace in Practice, but always there was a story or two that just knocked the wind out of them. Agnes sighed now and allowed a few moments of silence before she spoke.

"We've heard all three letters," she said, "and each of them brought back deep and painful memories that we can now start to deal with in our next few sessions. Many of us were hurt by strangers, but as you all heard, sometimes the greatest pain was inflicted by people we knew." Agnes paused and walked over to Tenneh.

"You did well, Tenneh," she said. "It hurts very much now because it's like you just put alcohol on your sore, but what does alcohol do?"

"The alcohol will make it get better," the girl answered, smiling at the simple analogy.

Agnes patted her on the shoulder and continued. "I know writing these letters was difficult, but what if you had to address the person who caused you such grief face to face? What if one day you saw the person who killed someone you loved?"

"I would kill him right then and there!" Rosetta said.

"And how would killing him bring about peace, Rosetta?" Agnes asked. "Where does the killing stop?"

"He should have thought about that before he killed my husband, Sis Agnes," Rosetta replied.

Josephine jumped in. "Me, I would just walk by and let it go. One day he will have to face God with his crimes."

"I'm sure there are some who would agree with Rosetta, and others who would agree with Josephine," Agnes said. "I want all of you to think about how you would deal with such a situation, and we'll discuss it at our next session."

"That's a good assignment, Sis Agnes," Tenneh said. "We the victims have a lot to say."

Agnes smiled kindly. "You're only a victim if you're dead, Tenneh," she said. "If we're still alive after all we went through," she told the group, "we are *survivors!*"

After the counseling session, Bendu went back to her office feeling a little down. She wrote a thank you note to Calvin, and then began working on a grant proposal for an income-generation project that would help PIP become sustainable. She immersed herself in the task, thankful to have something that would keep her mind off the sad thoughts elicited by Tenneh's letter. As a counselor it was not unusual to be moved by the clients, but Tenneh had a special place in Bendu's heart. Bendu liked the young girl's honesty and had never seen anyone else so grateful for PIP's services and so eager to repay the kindness to others even less fortunate than herself. That she could be so positive in light of what had happened to her was amazing.

The rest of the day went by quickly for Bendu, and, as usual, she and Agnes left the office together around 6 pm. It was still light outside, and the streets were busy with people trying to get back home before the 7 o'clock sundown. Agnes went to find a Congo Town taxi and Bendu decided to go get some bread from the Oriental Bakery on Mechlin Street before heading home. Several people greeted her by name as she walked down Broad Street: a couple of money changers, a woman selling bananas on the corner, and little Isaac, who, instead of going to school, made a living leading the blind man Boima around to beg. Boima chatted with her a bit, and she pressed a 50 LD note into his calloused hand before they parted.

Bendu turned left onto Mechlin Street and began to navigate the treacherous sidewalk, carefully dodging the mud and potholes. In her high heels and the long African print skirt that hugged her curves, it wasn't easy. As she passed the hair braiders who worked under cover of the damaged office building on Mechlin Street, one of them called out to her.

"Sister! Sister! You want your hair done? We can do a fine style for you!"

"Not today, thank you," Bendu replied, running her fingers through her short hair in a sudden moment of self-consciousness.

"Sis! We can come to your house if you're ashamed to do it outside!" a skinny young man shouted. The women around him laughed.

"I will let you know," Bendu yelled back, amused.

"Okay Sis, my name is Cyrus, you hear?" the skinny man said. "When you come, ask for me."

Bendu made it past the braiders and was almost past the Malag Clinic before she looked across the street at the gas station and saw something that stopped her cold. There, chatting with someone at the station, was Commander Cobra.

Bendu broke into a sweat and began to tremble. A painful knot formed in her stomach and she suddenly felt faint. She glanced in the direction of the gas station again. The sideburns were gone, but it was definitely him. She was sure. Suddenly, Cobra looked up and around, as if he felt someone looking at him. Bendu lowered her head, turned around, and walked quickly back toward Broad Street. She ducked into the dark space that must have once been the lobby of the damaged Mechlin Street office building. Besides the hair braiders, there were several other small businesses squatting there: a used-book seller, an African tie-and-dye dress seller, a woman cooking on coal-pots, and a man selling antique Liberian masks and other wood carvings. They all thought she wanted to buy something.

"No, no, no, please, no." Bendu waved them away and sat down on one of the large cement bricks lying around on the dirt floor. She lowered her head to get the blood flowing back to her brain, and the feeling of faintness began to subside. Images and sounds raced through her mind. Shouting, screaming, blood, gunfire, bodies, babies crying. Above it all, she thought she could hear her heart beating. Bendu closed her eyes and breathed deeply for a minute. When she had regained her composure she hurried back to the street and headed toward the gas station.

But Cobra was gone.

Chapter 5

For the second night in a row, Bendu woke up screaming and drenched in sweat. The dream was so vivid…

She was back in Duluma, being trained to fight. It was a sweltering day and she was on a routine drill with the other women from her room. They were jogging with their heavy rifles along their usual worn-out path when their leader suddenly made a sharp right turn and led them, still jogging, toward a large rusty zinc house half hidden behind some plum trees and hibiscus bushes in the distance. The leader brought them to a halt just before they reached the house. Commander Cobra appeared in the doorway, acknowledged their salute, and beckoned for the group to approach. They walked in single file and, after the blazing sun, their eyes needed time to adjust to the darkness in the windowless room. It only took a moment before out of the shadows rose a terrible sight. There, huddled in the middle of the floor, were about a dozen men. All of them were naked, tightly gagged, and tabayed—their elbows bound behind their backs. Lying in front of the frightened men was one who had been beheaded. The head lay on the ground, face frozen in terror. The knives and cutlasses used to kill him were lying on the ground beside the body, and there was blood everywhere—on the walls, seeping into the dirt, and on the hair and faces and bodies of those closest to him. Commander Cobra pulled Bendu and another woman out of the group and made them pick up the bloody weapons. "These are prisoners of war," he said. "You women—all of you—will execute them. We will show you how to do it." Muffled moaning rose from the desperate men on the ground as they began wriggling in vain attempts to free themselves. Commander Cobra scanned the group slowly and finally pointed to one of them. "That skull belongs to me," he said. The man's eyes widened in terror and he shook his head vigorously, struggling and making muffled sounds behind his gag as two fighters reached over and pulled him out to the front. Cobra gave a slight nod to his assistants, and one of them further disabled the poor trussed-up man with a blow to the back of the neck. Cobra grabbed the knife from Bendu, tilted his victim's head back, and sawed at his throat as if he were nothing but a goat. Blood gushed out and splashed all over Bendu and she screamed and screamed until there was nothing but blackness.

It was a warm night, but Bendu was shivering after the nightmare. The dream was just as terrifying as the day those executions actually took place. She felt her way to the bathroom, took a cup of cold water from the barrel, and washed her face. *That poor man. Was someone, somewhere, still looking for him?* She shook her head slowly. What if his family knew his skull had ended up being used as the top of a walking stick made for a warlord?

By the bright moonlight, Bendu studied her face in the mirror on the wall. Her large almond-shaped eyes looked tired and her curly afro was unkempt. "Lord, have mercy," she whispered, as she took the mirror down and placed it in the cabinet under the sink. She felt sick to her stomach. She had already missed a day of work, and she didn't know if she'd be able to go back in the morning. She had worked so hard to put the past behind her, but the mere sight of Commander Cobra had brought it all back in a matter of seconds.

As Bendu stumbled back to her room, she heard a loud knock at the gate. *Who could it be at this hour?* She glanced over at the clock on her bedside table and was surprised to see it was only 7:30 pm. The generator hadn't been turned on yet and it felt like the middle of the night. She had lost all track of time.

Now there was a knock on the front door. Bendu hesitated for a second. No, he couldn't possibly know where I live, she told herself. She made her way into the living room and the knock came again, this time accompanied by Agnes's voice calling out her name. Bendu breathed a sigh of relief and opened the door to see Agnes standing there with the old watchman who had let her in the gate. Bendu sent the watchman back to his post and stepped aside so Agnes could come in. Agnes was looking her up and down, and had a deep frown on her face.

Bendu looked down at herself. Her clothes were wrinkled and it was obvious she had slept in them.

"What's wrong Bendu? We're all worried! Why didn't you come to work?"

Bendu closed the door and leaned with her back against it. "I'm confused Agnes. I can't sleep. I feel sick."

"Why? What's going on?"

"A commander from the war. I saw him in town."

"Oh. Is that it?" Agnes turned and headed toward the sofa by memory. "Where's your lantern? I can't see."

"Wait. What do you mean 'Is that it?'"

Agnes kept on going. "I mean 'is that what's bothering you?'"

Bendu didn't answer. She found the lantern and matches on a shelf, raised the glass cover to expose the wick, and struck a match to light it. The room filled with a warm, golden glow and the smell of kerosene.

Agnes was already sitting down. "Come, sit down. When did you see this man?" she asked as Bendu approached.

"Two days ago."

"What's your connection with him?"

"It's Commander Cobra. He's the one that...captured me."

"Jesus." Agnes was speechless for a while. "Did he see you?" she finally asked.

Bendu shook her head.

"Well, if he didn't see you and he's not looking for you, there's no need to worry."

"That's not it."

"What is it then?"

Bendu frowned. "I'm not sure, exactly."

"You want me to stay here with you tonight?"

Bendu shook her head. "Thanks, but no. I'll be okay."

"Are you coming back to work?"

Bendu didn't answer.

"Are you afraid you'll run into him?"

Bendu frowned. "What's the chance of that?"

"Zero, but at least let me come for you in the morning," Agnes said. "We'll take a taxi together."

"Fine. Thanks, Agnes."

Agnes got up and scrutinized Bendu again. "Get some rest, you girl," she said, shaking her head. "There's nothing you can do to erase what happened."

As Bendu tossed and turned that night, questions kept running through her mind. Why was Cobra in town? Was he with the new group of rebels terrorizing Liberians in Lofa County? Why had she assumed he would never show his face in Liberia after the war? What was she going to do if she saw him again? "There's nothing you can do to erase what happened," Agnes had said. But wasn't that just an excuse for herself? Agnes had done some unspeakable things during the war, but had absolutely no feelings of remorse. 'Self-preservation is the first law of nature,' she always said whenever Bendu tried to make her see that feeling no guilt was just as unhealthy as drowning in self-pity. True, she couldn't erase what happened in Duluma, but was she just going to pretend it didn't happen? With those thoughts on her mind, and with help from the steady rain that started near midnight, Bendu eventually fell asleep.

Chapter 6

By the time the doorbell rang at 8 am, Bendu was already dressed and in a good mood. She was listening to *Monrovia This Morning* on DC 101 and packing up her papers and files for work.

Bendu opened the door with a smile and Agnes raised her eyebrows in surprise. "Is this the same person I talked to last night?" she asked.

Bendu pulled her into the house and closed the door. "Actually, no. I am *not* the same person," she replied.

"Oh?"

"Cobra's not going to ruin my life again. Nor anyone else's for that matter," she added as she slung her purse over her shoulder.

Agnes raised her eyebrows again. "And what do you mean by that?"

"He's going to pay for what he did to me, and for all the other atrocities he committed. I'm going to prosecute him for war crimes."

"Are you ready to go?"

Bendu opened the front door and they both stepped out. "I just told you I'm prosecuting Commander Cobra for war crimes and all you want to know is whether I'm ready to go?"

Agnes shrugged. "What do you want me to say Bendu? You of all people should know it's going to be impossible."

Bendu stopped in her tracks, wincing as if she had just been slapped. "And *you* of all people should be supporting me!"

Agnes ignored her and went over to the taxi she had chartered for one hour. The women rode together in the back seat with a wall of silence sitting between them.

Agnes spoke first as they walked up the two flights of stairs to Peace in Practice.

"I know you're vexed with me, but you know, I'm only trying to help you."

Bendu didn't answer.

Agnes paused a bit before she opened the office door. "I've asked Calvin and Siatta to help too."

"What!?" Bendu stared in disbelief at Calvin and her sister sitting in the waiting area. She turned and glared at Agnes. "What's wrong with you? Are you absolutely out of your mind?"

"This is serious Bendu. Let them help," Agnes whispered as Calvin and Siatta approached them anxiously. "They care about you."

"Last night you didn't seem to think it was so serious," Bendu retorted. She looked at Calvin and Siatta again, standing in front of her now. "I don't believe this."

Siatta returned to her seat and gathered her belongings in a huff. "Well, if our presence upsets you this much —"

Calvin turned back and grabbed Siatta's arm gently. "Wait," he urged. "Bendu needs family too, even if she can't see it now."

This time Bendu's rage was directed at Calvin. "How *dare* you talk about me as if I'm not even here? And as if I'm a child!"

Calvin walked over and put his arms around Bendu. She tried to move but he had her in a bear hug and wasn't letting her go. It was only when she stopped fighting that he stepped back.

"Okay, where do you want to talk?" he asked her gently.

"I guess we can all go to my office," she replied reluctantly, leading the way.

When they were settled, Calvin began asking her questions about Commander Cobra.

"What kind of car was he driving?"

"I don't know."

"Can you describe it?" Calvin asked. "Was it big? Small?"

"I don't remember."

"Did it have a trunk, or was it a station wagon? An SUV?"

Bendu squinted and shook her head. "I really can't remember now."

Calvin sighed. "I don't suppose you got the license plates."

"How could I?" Bendu almost shouted. "I wasn't close enough, but I was so shaken that even if I *was* close enough I don't think I would have been thinking about that."

Calvin nodded. "That's okay. I think our first priority should be to make sure you're protected. What's your cell phone number?"

"I stayed home yesterday, so I still don't have one."

"Okay, we'll get your phone and a number today. We'll also arrange security guards here at the office and at your house."

Bendu sat up straight. "No. First of all, Cobra's not looking for me. Second of all, *we* need to find *him*."

"Why?" Siatta wanted to know.

"I want to make sure he's brought to justice for what he did during the war."

Agnes looked at Bendu. "Is this a wise thing to do?"

"It's the right thing to do," Bendu answered.

"I already told her it's going to be impossible to get that man," Agnes said to Calvin and Siatta. "But her head is hard; she won't listen to me."

"Well maybe she *is* doing the right thing," Siatta said. "I don't know how all of you sat there and let illiterate ragtag hoodlums, fighters, and *children* rob, rape and kill you for so many years."

Now it was Agnes's turn to get angry. "I beg you, Siatta. Don't insult us. You people ran away to America. You were not here and you will *never* understand!"

"I guess I won't," Siatta retorted. "*I* would have stood up for myself and I would have refused to let anyone take my stuff, my dignity or my life."

Agnes's eyes narrowed and she shook her head. "'Would have, would have'. You have absolutely no idea what it was like and what you would have done —"

"Okay, okay, people..." Calvin interrupted. "This is not what we're here for." He turned back to Bendu. "Security is not an option. You may not think you need protection, but if he hears you're looking for him—well, you never know what might happen."

Bendu sighed and nodded reluctantly.

"Hey, maybe you could describe him for an artist to draw!" Siatta suggested.

Calvin laughed. "And do what?" he asked her. "Make a WANTED poster? No, we don't do that here Siatta. Don't worry, nobody can hide in Monrovia. We'll find him."

"Well, I hope we'll find him soon," Bendu said. "I can't even sleep at night, knowing he's somewhere out there."

"We know his war name, and surely somebody else will know exactly who we're talking about," Calvin said. "We'll find him. Don't worry. I'll take care of that."

Reassured, Bendu leaned back in her chair and relaxed a little.

"He had better not try anything foolish, that's all" Calvin added, "or he will have me to answer to!"

Bendu and Siatta glanced at each other.

"Calvin?" Siatta asked. "Is this about Benji?"

"Everything is about Benji," he answered.

"And what does getting Cobra have to do with Benji?" Agnes wanted to know.

Calvin didn't answer.

"He sees our brother's killer in every army guy," Siatta said.

"Well, that's not exactly true," Calvin said. "But in 1980 I stood by and watched those people torture and kill our family and friends and I was too young and powerless to do anything about it. I only knew one thing: that I would never let it happen again."

Agnes spoke up. "If this is why you want to find Cobra, I don't think it's a good thing," she said. "I would advise you not to do it."

"And why not?" Calvin asked. "Do you know what Bendu went through with this man?"

"Just be careful," Agnes warned. "It sounds like you want revenge."

"Don't worry," he replied. "All I want is justice. Same as you."

Chapter 7

Moses Varney waited for thirty minutes before the secretary finally ushered him into the Judiciary chambers for the second time that week.

The judge smiled when he saw his visitor. "V!"

Varney, seething inside for being made to wait so long—for no good reason, he was sure—forced himself to smile back. "Judge?"

Judge Dagoseh stood up and came around from behind his desk, grinning. "We're on it o!" he exclaimed, as if being "on it" was exhausting work.

On what? Varney wondered as he shook Solomon Dagoseh's hand. *A losing streak? A downward spiral? A crooked path?* Dagoseh was the most corrupt character in the justice department. And he was the only one who could help them. As they say, Varney reminded himself, sometimes you have to stand in poopoo to unclog the sewer.

Varney sat down and opened his bag. He still had qualms about what he was going to do. But how much longer could they wait for things to change? How much longer could they wait for promises to be kept? When would justice ever prevail if they didn't take action and establish it? Look at his driver Weah. All the young man wanted was an opportunity to make a good life for himself, but archaic land and labor systems in his village, and unfair systems in the country as a whole, had led him to choose the life of a combatant as his way out. What kind of choice was that?

Varney looked at the contents of his bag. This one payment to Dagoseh would take care of several things: manpower for the cause, security for getting supplies to their people, and, when all was said and done, the power that they needed to finally change the living and working conditions of the poorest Liberians. For a start, they would fix up the deplorable schools, create better housing, and provide good jobs. Varney thought about how his father had once worked on a farm where the owner trapped most of the workers by giving them goods from his store on credit. At months' end they often had no wages and sometimes even owed their employer money. Where was the protection for those people? Where was the justice? Probably in the greasy palms of someone like the man in front of him.

Dagoseh leaned back in his armchair—his big belly rising too far above his desk. Varney took note of it as he stacked the bundles of money on the desk. He had to fight to keep himself from throwing the bundles at Dagoseh's head. This man represented all that was wrong with Liberia, and here he was wielding power in the courthouse of all places.

Varney and the judge went a long way back, but at some point had taken different paths based on their respective definitions of redemption: while Varney saw it as liberation of the people from tyranny, Dagoseh saw it as liberation of himself from poverty.

The judge was swiveling from side to side now, in his large office chair. Varney placed the last bundle on the stack and watched as Dagoseh swept his thirty pieces of silver into the desk drawer and locked it. At least he's embarrassed enough not to count it, Varney thought, as the judge rose from his chair and grabbed a manila envelope from on the desk. Dagoseh came around, and handed the envelope to Varney on their way to the door.

"Thanks for your help," Varney said, clutching the bulky envelope under his arm.

Dagoseh patted him on the back. "No problem man. Glad to be a part of the revolution."

Varney wanted to slap him.

Chapter 8

True to his word, Calvin was relentless in his search for Commander Cobra. Siatta had asked Terrance to help too, what with all his connections. But Terrance had refused, citing reluctance to use his influence that way.

For several days and nights, rain or shine, Calvin inquired at popular hotels, bars, and nightclubs, and used every development or "no development" as an excuse to call Bendu. She was touched by his attention and probably would have been amused had the circumstances not been so serious.

As the days went by, Bendu, with encouragement and support from Siatta and Agnes, resumed her normal activities. She still found it hard to look at herself in the mirror though, and the nights were still bad, as the nightmares refused to go away. One nightmare that kept coming back was the one about her failed attempt to escape from Duluma. Thankfully, she always managed to wake up before she had to face Cobra and Samson. As frightening as they were though, she found the nightmares useful; they brought back details she had started to forget, and they strengthened her resolve to press charges against Cobra if he was ever found.

About a week after she first saw Cobra, Bendu and Siatta went to Calvin's place off Tubman Boulevard in Congo Town for what he had promised would be a relaxing afternoon by the pool. When they got there, he was already in his swimming trunks and a grey T-shirt with the letters FBI on it. He greeted them both warmly and led them through a brightly lit foyer decorated with life-sized wooden carvings of animals and of Africans frozen in the usual roles: woman with baby on her back, hunter with bow and arrow and a deer slung over his shoulders, woman carrying a basket of something on her head. The living room was a tasteful bachelor's space: simple black leather furniture, coffee- and end-tables made of mahogany and glass, and artwork framed by ïmageafrica on the wall behind the sofa. A giant stereo system stood against another wall, surrounded by what looked like a thousand CDs. Directly across the room from the stereo was a sliding glass door which Calvin opened to let them outdoors to the pool.

Bendu and Siatta went into the changing area to put on their swimsuits. They soon settled down in lounge chairs to enjoy the jazz Calvin had put on. A servant brought them soft drinks and a large bottle of Club Beer, and, after a bit of happy reminiscing about some of the fun they had had as teenagers, the conversation turned to their current lives. But eventually, as Siatta began to ask about old friends from the past, they began to talk about the unpleasant but unavoidable topic of the war. So many people they knew were in exile, and so many others were simply missing, including a whole football team they used to sponsor.

"I'm sure we'll find those boys somewhere," Siatta said.

Calvin shook his head as he sat up and poured himself another glass of cold beer. "Highly unlikely."

Siatta sat up too. "Why do you say that?" she asked.

"Because it's true," he answered. "Boys and men were often killed systematically. No warring faction wore uniforms so you didn't know whose side anyone was on. Every faction feared men that they didn't know."

Siatta was incredulous. "So they would just kill any man?"

"Very often, yes," Calvin told her. "Unless someone around knew you and could vouch for you, that was it." He took a long drink and lay down again.

Bendu nodded in agreement. "Or unless you had special skills," she added. "Many young men thought it was better to join a faction. That way they wouldn't be among the targeted and powerless civilians."

Siatta, who had their mother's light skin, rubbed some sunscreen on her legs and arms. "I've heard so many terrible stories since I came back home," she said. "Men, women, children—everyone's been so traumatized."

Calvin put his hands behind his head, chest now bare so he could soak up the often elusive Rainy Season sun. "I'm sorry," he said, "but their war stories don't move me one bit. Displacement, starvation, whatever... I don't care. I don't feel sorry for any of those people."

Bendu pushed her sunglasses up onto her head and turned to look at him. "'Those people' Calvin?"

"You know who I'm talking about," he answered, without returning her gaze. "The tender mercies —"

"But they were victims, Calvin!" Siatta interrupted. "Especially the women and children. They're not the ones who committed the crimes."

"And how do you know?" Calvin asked, a bit more expressively now. "How do you know what the women and children did to make it through the war?"

Siatta paused to think about it.

"Some of the most vicious killers during the war were women," Calvin went on. "The sweetest, most gentle-looking women didn't think twice about castrating a man or cutting someone's throat."

Bendu put her sunglasses back on and her mind flew to Agnes, a.k.a. Mama Don't Care.

"So, everyone 'did what they had to do?'" Siatta asked.

"That's right," Calvin said, rising to his feet. "Even the children joined factions and took up arms. Especially children who were orphaned by the war and had nowhere else to turn. It was all about survival. I'm going for a swim. Anyone care to join me?"

"And what did *you* have to do, Calvin?" Siatta called after him. "Did you have to kill people too?"

But Calvin dove into the water without answering.

Bendu glanced sideways at Siatta. Siatta was looking straight at her and Bendu was glad her eyes were hidden behind the dark shades. She adjusted her lounge chair to get a better view of Calvin swimming. He had reached the other side with powerful freestyle strokes, and was returning with a graceful breaststroke.

"Bendu?"

Siatta's voice was so small, Bendu wasn't sure she had been called until she saw the waiting look on Siatta's face.

"Bendu, did *you* ever…kill someone?"

Before Bendu could say anything, Calvin rose up out of the water and picked up where he had left off before his dip in the pool. "You know what? After what they did to us in 1980,

I almost want to say they deserved everything they got," he said, drying his face with a big white towel as he walked over. "And don't tell me it was their grandparents and parents who rejoiced in the streets when President Tolbert and all those cabinet ministers and officials were killed. I don't care. I'll never forget how those ungrateful people tortured us or how they killed Benji." Then he turned and yelled in the direction of the house: "David! Bring some ice and more drinks!"

"Calvin, listen to yourself," Bendu said gently, shocked that he could be so cold-hearted.

Calvin sat down and looked from one sister to the other. "What?"

"You sound like…"

"Like what? Do you know their so-called intellectuals are blaming the deaths from the war on Congo people?"

"That's ridiculous," Siatta said.

"Ridiculous but true," said Calvin, drying off the rest of his body. "They say in 1980 they killed 13 of us, and then *we* turned around and killed 200,000 of *them*."

Siatta frowned. "Wasn't most of the killing done by native people?"

"What can I say? Those who were there saw the people who did it. I challenge anyone to point out a Congo man who they saw killing somebody because they belonged to Tribe A or Tribe B. They killed each other—plain and simple. David is coming; ask him."

"People killed for all kinds of reasons," Bendu explained to her sister. "Hatred, jealousy, revenge, self defense, you name it. Sometimes they killed just to prove they were tough or just to instill fear in the people around them. It's almost impossible to find people who fought for any kind of ideology."

"In the beginning maybe," Siatta said.

Calvin spoke up again. "In the beginning there *was* a purpose: get the President out. Ten years of Doe were enough and the repression was only getting worse. Once he was out though, everyone just went crazy! They've destroyed this country...destroyed it!"

"Well, everyone has to take a little bit of the blame for where we were then, and for where we are now," Bendu said. "Come on Siatta—our turn; the water looks good."

Siatta perked up. "Oh no. First of all, I'm not getting my hair wet. Second of all, I'm not taking the blame for anything," she said. "*I* have done nothing wrong. No individual should be punished for the sins of their ancestors."

Later that evening, when Bendu was back in her house, Siatta's words resonated with her. She kept hearing them over and over again: *I'm not taking the blame for anything. I have done nothing wrong.* The questions that often plagued her came back too. What if her friends and family found out what had happened to her, or what she had done? Would they understand? Would they forgive her? Bendu said the words aloud: "I'm not taking the blame for anything. I have done nothing wrong." She stopped and sighed. *Who am I fooling?* she asked herself.

When it started to get dark, Bendu lit several candles and placed them around the small house that she maintained for an exiled family in lieu of paying rent. It was a far cry from the stately home she had grown up in, but it was enough for her. She was happy as long as she had food to eat and a roof over her head. There was no need for any extras, especially in a time like this. The neighbor's generator wouldn't be coming on until 7 pm, and then she would have current for five hours for the $50 US a month she paid to help with the fuel. Not too bad, except in the last couple of weeks they kept putting the generator on later and later, and twice it didn't come on at all.

Bendu had brought work home from the office, but that night, by the time the current came on, she was lying in bed thinking of something else Siatta had said: *No individual should be punished for the sins of their ancestors.* Bendu lay under her light covers and for the first time since she had seen Cobra in town, she allowed herself to think at length about her life with the fighters.

Chapter 9

The morning after the fighters dragged Bendu Lewis away with them, leaving her grandmother dead by the roadside, Commander Cobra woke up, rolled a giant *dujee*, and smoked it while he cleaned his gun. The scent of the marijuana brought a couple of new young fighters wandering over near his tent where they loitered rather noisily, hoping to be thrown a stash for themselves. Drugs were plentiful within almost all the factions of the Liberian civil war, and leaders were known to distribute them liberally among their troops. Cobra reassembled his weapon, loaded it, then went outside and tested it on the two unlucky men. They didn't even have time to beg for their lives.

The shots brought everyone out. Even Bendu, with her left hand swollen to twice its size and throbbing with pain, came outside to see what the commotion was about. Commander Cobra took a deep drag of his dujee, scanned the scattered group of onlookers slowly, and went back into his tent. While everyone was still paralyzed with fear and uncertainty, he popped his head out and bellowed to no one in particular:

"When I come out again these two men better be gone!" With that, he disappeared again and everyone began scurrying about. Four men grabbed their dead comrades and began carrying them out of the camp, women began sweeping and making preparations for the midday meal, and a co-ed group dressed in jeans, white T-shirts and black berets were led jogging and singing to a nearby field.

Bendu looked around and saw that the thirty or so fighters who had taken her were actually part of a larger group. There were about a hundred people outside now, and probably more who had chosen to remain in their shelters. From the look of the place—clothes hanging on lines, several cooking spots with a considerable amount of ash accumulated—she figured the camp had been lived-in for some time. In fact it looked like it was built around an abandoned village for there were quite a few small mud structures, and one large concrete structure that had been burnt out. The place was deep in the woods and she had no idea which way the main road was or how long it would take to get to it.

She went back into the large mud house where she had been nursed throughout the night by Hannah—one of the young women she had seen among the group the night before—and an older woman who was showered with affection by everyone who came around. They called her Ma Musu. She was 54 years old, but people only knew her age because she told them. She had bright friendly eyes and a radiant smile that showed perfectly straight white teeth. But even she was subdued now by what the commander had done.

"Why did he kill those men?" Bendu asked her. "What did they do?"

"I don't know, my daughter," Ma Musu replied. "Those are his ways. When a Cobra bites you...hmmm! Cobra will strike anyone. But let me tell you: among all the leaders he is one of the most disciplined. Everybody's scared of him, but they respect him too. Come, let me see that hand."

Bendu went closer to Ma Musu and held out her hand. Hannah was among the co-ed group going for exercise and drills, so the two of them were alone now. The woman began rubbing a green paste all over her arm, starting from her elbows. The smell of it reminded Bendu of blue cheese. She yelled and writhed in pain when Ma Musu began to massage her hand and fingers, but the woman, who often tended to trauma that was much worse, paid no attention to her cries.

"That boy broke all your fingers," she said. "Wicked! Wicked people! Just wait until I see him."

To Bendu's surprise and relief, the pain soon began to subside.

"You mustn't let Cobra scare you," Ma Musu said quietly. "They say he does these things just to look tough, so nobody can mess with him. He's a good man, but when he's smoking his drugs, it's a whole different story. He completely loses his mind and sometimes he won't even remember what he did."

"Really?"

"You will see. Tomorrow he might ask for these same two boys that he killed. Then when they tell him what he did to them he will get weak and feel bad."

"That's crazy!"

Ma Musu looked up from her rubbing. "War makes you crazy my child. War makes all of us crazy."

"Ma Musu, where are we?" Bendu asked.

"They call this place Duluma."

"How far is it from Monrovia?"

"I don't know, my daughter."

"Are you from this area?"

"I came here from near Totota. We were running away from our village when they captured some of us and brought us here. Now keep closing your hand and opening it, like this." Ma Musu demonstrated and Bendu obeyed.

"You were with your family?" Bendu asked.

"I was with my sister and two of my daughters. By that time they had killed my husband and taken my two sons."

How come it's always 'they?' Bendu thought. *They killed... they stole...they say...* "Who killed your husband, Ma Musu? Who?"

Ma Musu shrugged and began packing up her medicines and herbs. "They say one young boy did it. When the soldiers came I wasn't there. I was on the farm with the other women. When we got back the whole village was *chakla*—everything scattered and destroyed. Almost all our men were dead or gone. They only left the old people and the small children."

"And you don't know where your sons are?"

"No, my child. I only pray that one day God will let me see them again."

Ma Musu closed the small medicine bag and the two sat in silence for a while.

"How about your sister and your daughters?" Bendu finally asked. "Where are they now?"

"My sister died on the 4th of March from cholera. My daughters are here, at Duluma. You've already met Hannah, the elder of the two. You girl, you're asking plenty questions!" Ma Musu's smile returned, but then Bendu saw her brow furrow.

"And you, where are your people?" Ma Musu asked, curious.

"They're in the States."

"Your Ma and Pa?"

"Yes. They left in 1990."

"And how did you and your grandmother get lost from her people in Sumoville? Hannah told me that's where you were."

Bendu spoke quietly as she told Ma Musu about their ordeal:

They had been spending some time with her grandmother's cousin, Rebecca Johnson. On the day before they were supposed to leave Sumoville and head back to town, they heard the rebels were close by. Cousin Rebecca decided she and her children and grandchildren would stay right there where they were, in the family compound where they had lived all their lives. They wanted Bendu and Granny May to stay too, especially since Granny May was not well. But Bendu had insisted that if they left very early in the morning, while it was still dark, they would somehow make it back to Monrovia. They had been in Sumoville for two weeks, and while she enjoyed spending time in the interior with her grandmother's relatives, she was ready to get back to the excitement of city life.

The next day, her cousin Orlando, despite his grandmother's pleas, escorted them to the place where the minibuses and taxis picked people up for rides to Monrovia and other cities and towns along the way. The place was deserted and as they were deliberately early, they assumed they were simply the first ones to arrive. There was no real shelter at the parking spot, just a couple of bamboo benches built under the shade of a large plum tree, so that's where they settled down to wait. As the minutes crept by, Orlando began to feel uneasy and urged them to start heading back to the house.

Bendu was reluctant to turn back, and even Granny May didn't feel like walking the distance again. Her hip hurt, she had a headache, and the bunion on her foot was becoming more and more painful. "Child, you just get me back to Dr. Freeman," she said. "He's the only one can fix this ol' body."

As the minutes turned into an hour, then two, Granny May developed a fever and all of them began to regret leaving the safety of the village. Just then they heard several vehicles approaching at such high speed that they knew it couldn't be public transportation. They hurried to hide in the nearby woods—as quickly as they could with Granny May in tow—but someone in the first car of the passing convoy spotted them, and the vehicles screeched to a halt. There were five in all: two camouflaged jeeps, two pick-ups, and one private car—a station wagon.

"Were they government soldiers?" Ma Musu asked.

"I don't know," Bendu said. "But the two pick-ups were full of young boys and men with no shirts on, and they all had their hands and feet tied up."

There were no questions asked. The men in the jeeps jumped out quickly, grabbed Orlando, ripped his shirt off him, tied him up and threw him into the back of one of the pick-ups. The two women were led to the car and ushered in. It all happened so fast there was no time to react.

The convoy was obviously in a big hurry. They drove at high speed for almost an hour. During that time someone in "Jeep One" occasionally called the driver of the car on his handset. She had listened attentively, but the two men talked mostly in code. It sounded like they were referring to compass positions, directions, and places she had never heard of. The only thing she managed to decipher was that the Diana Bridge had been destroyed. That explained the lack of public transportation.

The other people in the station wagon were a mixed group of men, women, and children. Perhaps they were relatives being taken to safety by the men in the convoy, she thought. No one said a word to each other though, and the tension was high. Bendu had looked intently at the landscape as they drove by, to see if she would spot a sign or a landmark that would tell her where they were. It was hopeless. For miles and miles there was nothing but trees and bush—unused, wasted land in a nation inhabited by hungry people.

Ma Musu put a comforting hand on Bendu's shoulder. "So where did they take you?"

"When we got to Charlue Town they took me and Granny May out of the car and told us they were keeping my cousin Orlando. We begged them to give him back to us but they refused. Orlando was crying like a baby. I keep thinking about Cousin Rebecca, and how she didn't want him to take us to the bus station."

Ma Musu shook her head sadly. She had tears in her eyes too, and Bendu knew she must be thinking of her sons.

The people of Charlue Town had given them shelter, she told Ma Musu, but Charlue Town was a small village—not really a town at all—and there was no medical care for Granny May. Her fever got worse and she said it felt like she had malaria. By the end of the first week she had lost a lot of weight and could hardly walk. Food was scarce and Bendu didn't want to impose too much on the poor villagers, so she too started to get thinner. By the end of their second week in Charlue Town, Granny May could not get out of bed. Her eyes and cheeks were sunken in and she was often delirious, talking to people from her past. And then the attack came and got them all fleeing.

Bendu paused and wondered how the others had fared. Were they hiding in the woods? Did they reach a safe town?

"Ay God, no!" Ma Musu exclaimed suddenly, startling Bendu out of her thoughts.

"What is it Ma Musu?"

The woman had noticed something disturbing at the window. Someone. They heard footsteps, then a loud knock at the door. Ma Musu quickly ushered Bendu toward the mat where she had slept, using signs to indicate that she should lie down and keep quiet.

A man shouted "Ma Musu!" Then came more knocks.

"I'm coming Joseph, let me tie my lappa," the woman answered, even though the faded fabric was already wrapped snugly around her waist. She looked to see that Bendu was down, then she opened the door just wide enough to poke her head out. Bendu peeked from under the covers. There was an armed man there with Joseph.

"Yes?" Ma Musu asked them quietly.

"Ay Ma Musu," said Joseph, grinning nervously. He glanced at Bendu on the floor. "You know what we came for."

"But the girl is sick."

"The chief sent for her."

"She's resting. Whole night she didn't sleep, after what Samson did to her hand."

"Ma Musu, you want to get me in trouble with my Bossman?"

Before she could answer, the other man stepped forward, grabbed Ma Musu by the arm and pushed her out of the doorway. "Look, you woman!" he growled. "Don't give us a hard time today!"

Bendu rose to her feet quickly and placed herself between Ma Musu and the aggressive man, arms akimbo. "You don't push Ma Musu," she said evenly, challenging him with her eyes.

The man's eyes widened and he gripped his gun more tightly. Bendu stood there with her hands on her hips, and for a moment she thought he was about to lunge at her. But then he took a step back and wrenched his eyes away from her steady gaze to peer over her shoulder at the older woman.

"Sick or not, sleeping or not, the chief sent for her, Ma," he said quietly.

"Is he in the oven?" Ma Musu asked.

Bendu frowned. *The oven?*

"He's in his room," Joseph answered.

"O thank God," Ma Musu whispered, gently ushering Bendu toward the door.

The men led Bendu to their commander's tent, where Samson, the one who had broken her fingers, sat on guard outside. He was wearing only his black army pants tucked into combat boots, and the muscles of his arms and chest rippled as he sharpened a large knife. His shoulder length dreadlocks were large and matted, and made him look like a madman. Bendu's heart pounded with fear and rage when she saw him, but he was already high on something and paid no special attention to her.

Joseph opened the flap of the tent and pushed the frightened girl inside gently. Commander Cobra had finished his dujee, but the scent of it still permeated the stuffy air in there. He was fiddling with some communication equipment and didn't even bother to look up at her. After a long uncomfortable silence he finally spoke.

"So, tell me why you insulted us last night, Miss Lewis."

Bendu had to think for a moment before she realized he was talking about the way she had sucked her teeth at the fighters when they first saw her.

"I didn't mean to —"

"There's no place for disrespect in this group."

"Yes sir."

"You're lucky we didn't kill you." Cobra went on testing the equipment and Bendu's heart raced as she wondered what her fate *would* be.

"There are many factions around this area. You'll stay here with us, where you'll be safe."

"Yes sir. Thank you, sir." She breathed a sigh of relief and realized her death wish had passed. She wanted to stay alive. She *had* to stay alive.

Cobra looked at her for the first time since she entered his tent. "Women are very important at the battlefront. You will make yourself useful while you are here."

"What can I do sir?"

Cobra chuckled. "Samson!" he called.

The man entered the tent immediately. "Yes, chief!"

"She wants to make herself useful, so I'm deploying her. Take her. She's your new wife."

Samson laughed. "Cobra strikes again! Thank you, chief."

"We need your strength, so just make sure she doesn't cut your hair," the commander joked. They both laughed this time, as Bendu stood there stunned, speechless, paralyzed, unable to believe she had just been given away like a piece of property by someone acting as if he owned her.

Samson pulled her outside and placed the knife at her throat. "You make noise, you give me a hard time, I will cut your throat. Let's go!" He led her through the camp at knifepoint and her face burned with shame as everyone stared. Despite his threat, it was a struggle just for her to put one foot in front of the other, and Samson had to half drag her along. *Help me, somebody,* she prayed in her heart. But no one came to her rescue. Some of the women in the yard averted their eyes, and some shook their heads sadly, trying to communicate some sympathy with their motions. But no one dared say anything out loud.

A quiet hush fell over the yard as they entered Samson's hut, and Bendu tried not to cry aloud when he pushed her on to his filthy mattress, tore off her clothes, and began to rape her. She kept her broken fingers and sore arm out of his way and prayed silently for deliverance. Through her tears she spied his knife on the little stool next to his bed. It glinted in the sliver of sunlight that entered through the wooden slats at the window. Glinted and beckoned to her. But she could never kill anyone, she thought, not even now with the possibility of getting HIV from this monster.

In the course of the year Bendu would indeed kill, but she didn't know that now, and was still horrified at the evil she saw all around her. In her, now, panting and sweating, grunting like an animal, using her like an object. A voice began screaming in her head. Bendu suddenly became hysterical and began hitting Samson's face over and over again as hard as she could with her good hand. She managed to give him one strong blow to the eye before he subdued her by grabbing her by the wrists and pinning her down with her hands above her head. Even as his eye throbbed and oozed blood from one corner as it swelled shut, he continued to violate her and she no longer worried about keeping quiet for the neighbors' sake; she wailed as if he was taking her very life, piece by precious piece.

Chapter 10

The pepperbirds stirred Bendu out of her sleep with their chirping, but she kept her eyes closed, and in a moment of confusion, tried to remember where she was. Then she heard a familiar voice calling somewhere in the neighborhood, "Tide soap? Washing soap? Blue?" She smiled with relief. The *yana boy* was wandering through the neighborhood selling his soap and bleach as he did six days a week, and she was home in Monrovia—not in Duluma with Samson. Bendu kept her eyes closed and said a quick prayer of thanksgiving.

Later in the morning, after she had had breakfast and picked some fresh flowers for the tables, Bendu headed to the nearby supermarket. And for the second time that morning, she heard a familiar voice calling. This one was calling her name, and the voice was unmistakable.

"Miss Lewis!"

She froze.

"Miss Lewis!" the voice shouted again, from much closer this time.

Bendu spun around to the direction from which the voice was coming. There, crossing the street and coming toward her, was Commander Cobra. Bendu's eyes darted about, scanning the area quickly. There were about three or four people sitting on the sidewalk, selling biscuits, candy, candles and other small things from wooden trays. *Witnesses!*

Cobra reached her side of the street and Bendu took a step back. He strode toward her, his big muscular frame looming closer and closer.

Bendu's heart was racing. She took another step back, stumbling over a large crack in the sidewalk. *Thank God the supermarket is just half a block away*, she thought; *they'll hear me if I scream.*

Cobra stopped, peered at Bendu, and broke into a grin. "Lieutenant TKO!" he said, greeting her by her *nom de guerre.* "Is that you? Is that really you?"

Before she could respond he reached out and hugged her as if they were old friends. "It's so good to see you again!"

Bendu was stunned.

Cobra placed a heavy hand on her shoulder. "How have you been?" he asked.

"Fine," she replied, her voice shaking even on just the one syllable.

He stepped back and looked her up and down slowly. "You're certainly *looking* fine," he said. "We should get together sometime soon and catch up with each other. Especially since you left us so...unexpectedly," he added with an accusing glance.

Inside, Bendu was seething with an emotion she couldn't quite name. But she kept her cool and forced a shaky smile.

"You want to get together for a drink while I'm in town?" Cobra asked.

She was about to say no, then thought better of it. "Tell me where to find you."

"I'm at El Meson on Carey Street," he said, pulling a slip of paper out of his wallet.

While Cobra wrote down his room and phone numbers, Bendu gripped her purse tightly, as if to gain some support from it. "Please don't ever call me by that war name again," she said quietly, but firmly.

Commander Cobra smiled and handed Bendu the slip of paper. "You're still cheeky, but you're right," he said. "We should put all that behind us. But I swear, you girl, I will never forget the way Samson's eye looked that day after you punched him. TKO—a Technical Knock-Out!" He laughed and punched her on the shoulder playfully.

Bendu could only look at him.

He cocked his head and looked at her with a question in his eyes, but this time she couldn't fake an amiable response. Had he forgotten how she became involved with Samson at all that first day in Duluma?

He cleared his throat. "Well, Miss Lewis...Oh, is it still Miss Lewis? Or is it Mrs. Something now?"

Bendu looked down at her feet and suppressed the urge to knock *him* out. "Miss Lewis," she answered. *How could he act so...normal?*

"All right Miss Lewis. I'm surprised no one has married you yet. I wish I could stay and talk some more, but I have some business to take care of. I'm serious, let's get together soon okay?"

She managed a slight nod. "Goodbye Commander Cobra."

The man who had ruined her life chuckled and shook his head. "No, no, babe. I forgot to tell you," he said. "I go by the name Moses Varney these days. When you come, just ask for V."

Bendu held on to the slip of paper he had given her, and watched him go until he was out of sight. *V*, she thought with contempt. *Vile, vicious animal.*

Chapter 11

~~~

Moses Varney at El Meson on Carey Street. Calvin was ready to pounce. Bendu had gone by his house to tell him the news. Siatta was almost as eager to take action as Calvin, and said she was in the neighborhood and would come over to join them right away. Agnes was in a taxi when Bendu called.

"We know where he is!" Bendu blurted out when she heard her friend's voice.

"Who?"

"Cobra! Who else?"

"Oh."

Bendu stopped her pacing.

"Bendu just leave that man alone," Agnes said. "Why did you go hunting for him?"

"I didn't. He walked up to me on the street."

"You see? When you're not looking for trouble, trouble always comes to find you."

Bendu smiled. Agnes. She had a saying or an analogy for every occasion.

"And so what are you going to do now?" Agnes wanted to know.

"I don't know. We're here to come up with a plan and we need you." Bendu noticed Calvin glance over at her impatiently.

"To tell you the truth…" Agnes's voice trailed off.

"You didn't want me to find him."

"You'll only cause trouble for yourself. I know you."

"And I thought *I* knew *you*."

"I just don't want you to get hurt, Bendu."

Bendu rolled her eyes. "What more can he do to me? Agnes please come. Let me give you the directions to Calvin's place. Where are you right now?"

"Actually I'm getting ready to go visit Tenneh."

"Tenneh?"

"She's in the hospital. They took her in this morning."

"Oh no! What happened?" She saw Calvin look up again, eyebrows furrowed with concern this time.

"We don't know. Maybe they'll tell us something when we get there. Her sister came to the sewing class this morning to let us know. She said Tenneh had a bad cough and they think it might be TB."

Bendu frowned and headed back toward the living room. "Fine. Go see Tenneh and let me know what they say."

Bendu hung up just as Siatta pulled into the yard in her little silver Mercedes. Calvin went to open the door and Bendu plopped herself down on the sofa. It was a good thing she knew Agnes well. Somewhere in there, the woman did have a heart. Just the fact that she had taken in two war orphans and one child who was separated from his parents was proof enough. Agnes wasn't being too supportive now, but Bendu understood why.

"So, what are you going to do now that you've found Cobra?" Siatta asked Bendu after they had all settled down around the coffee table. "Notify the DA?"

Calvin laughed. "The DA? Siatta, there's no District Attorney here."

"How can that be? Who prosecutes crimes?" she asked.

"The Liberian justice system is not exactly up to speed," Bendu informed her sister. "We'll have to go directly to the police station and see if we can have Cobra arrested and sent to jail."

"How soon?"

"It's Saturday. Maybe even today." She turned to Calvin. "Are you free?"

"I am, but I don't want to waste my time with the police. I want to take care of this myself."

Bendu frowned. "What do you mean?"

"Look, they're just going to give you the run-around. Half of these guys are war-time buddies."

"I thought you said you weren't interested in revenge."

"Well, I'm not interested in wasting my time either."

"And what exactly do you want to do when you confront Mr. Varney?" Siatta asked him.

"Besides kill him? I'm not sure yet."

"Hhmm. Well, *I* want to do this the right way," Bendu said.

Calvin smirked. "You go ahead then," he said. "Go right ahead. Let's see where the right way will get you."

Bendu couldn't tell whether he was mad or joking. "So you're deserting me?"

Calvin stood up and jingled his keys in his pocket. "No—I'll give you a ride to the station. What are you ladies having to drink?"

"Nothing for me," Bendu answered.

Siatta shook her head. "Me neither."

Calvin went to the kitchen and Bendu turned to her sister. "Siatta? Are you deserting me too?"

"Well, I don't think I can handle your police station, but I'll ride with Calvin."

"You people are hopeless! I can't believe this. Now that we know where the guy is, you're backing out?"

"Look —" Siatta began.

"No, never mind. It's fine. Let it stay. I'll call Agnes again."

Bendu got up and went outdoors with her cell phone. Agnes answered right away.

"Can you go visit Tenneh this evening?" Bendu asked. "I need you now, before the police station closes. They're only open until 2 on Saturdays and I want to go there right now —"

"Wait! Slow down. What's going on?"

Bendu took a deep breath and exhaled slowly. "I need you Agnes. I need you to be there with me when I tell the police about Cobra. Today."

There was a long silence as Agnes pondered the request.

"Are you there?"

"Yes. What about Calvin? Or your sister?"

"I need *you*, Agnes. Even though you don't think I should prosecute...well, I know *you* understand that this is what I need to heal."

This time the silence was shorter. "Where should I meet you?" her friend asked.

Chapter 12

⁓

Bendu could tell that Lieutenant James Tarpeh was not too happy to be disturbed on a Saturday afternoon.

In fact, Tarpeh was looking forward to going home early like the rest of the staff, but he thought it was interesting that he was now in a position to grant or deny Benjamin Lewis's daughter a favor.

The office assistant had told Bendu and Agnes that Lieutenant Tarpeh would be happy to see them. Bendu held her head up high now, and smiled sweetly. For once she was going to reap the benefits of having connections without feeling an ounce of guilt about it.

Lieutenant Tarpeh frowned when he heard what the two women wanted. "Have him arrested for *what?*" he asked incredulously.

"Murder," Bendu repeated.

Lieutenant Tarpeh took a handkerchief out of his pocket and wiped the sweat off his face before he looked up again at the two women. He was a nondescript man, his new as-yet-unfaded uniform and extra insignia the only things that distinguished him from the men he led.

"And what if he denies the charges? How do you intend to prove he killed anybody?"

"I'm not the only one who knows him. Others will come forward; we just have to start by getting his name and photo out there."

"That's what you think? It's not going to be that easy, sweetheart," the police lieutenant warned. "First of all, no judge will issue—within the required 48 hours—the documents necessary to keep this man in prison."

"Why? Is that not enough time?"

Tarpeh shook his head. "Honestly? Even if the judge had a month he wouldn't do it. No one in any high position in this administration is going to put anyone away for war crimes."

"And why not?"

"That's not our priority right now. We're not getting paid and we've got staff looking to us for *their* salaries. I just don't see this pursuit going anywhere."

"So what do you suggest we do? Let Mr. Varney go free?" Agnes asked.

"At least for now, yes."

"What do you mean by 'at least for now'?" Bendu wanted to know.

"Well —" His voice trailed off.

"Are you hoping I'll change my mind or give up?"

"I'm just saying this: Tensions are high right now, and the security situation is not good. The rebels are getting closer and —"

"You want me to wait until the rebels are pushed back? How long will that take? Then what?"

"Bendu, calm down," Agnes whispered softly.

"No!" Bendu said to her loudly, without taking her eyes off Tarpeh. "Will I have to wait until the economy is back on track and people have been paid too?" she asked him. "By then the man will be long gone! You know that."

"Look, darling, it's for your own safety," Tarpeh said.

"Thanks for your advice," Bendu said, "but with all due respect, I can't let him escape. Not now."

Lieutenant Tarpeh shrugged. "Fine, love. What is this man's full name?" he asked, opening his ledger to a clean page.

"Moses Varney."

"Moses Varney." He tried to write the name down but there was no ink in the pen. He scribbled near the bottom of the page, but to no avail. "Do you have a pen I can borrow?"

Bendu handed him a pen.

Moses Varney, he wrote. "And when did he commit this murder?"

"Murders. In the early 1990s."

"The date—oh, excuse me, *dates*—please."

Bendu glared at him. "It was during the war. Mainly in 1991, if I have to give you a specific year."

The lieutenant smirked. "Do you have the names of the victims?"

"He killed lots of people."

Tarpeh stopped writing and moved only his eyes to look up.

"That's fine, I just need their names."

"He killed lots of people. I don't have their names."

Lieutenant Tarpeh sighed like he was bored. "All right. Lots of people? How many people would you say?

"I don't know."

"*Around* how many?" he asked.

Bendu didn't answer.

Lots of people, Tarpeh wrote, saying the words aloud as he wrote them. Bendu winced.

"Listen, you can make fun of us all you want," Agnes said, "but I'm telling you—this Moses Varney is a dangerous man. He's a criminal!"

"And *I'm* telling *you*: if you want to arrest him it must be for a specific murder and you must have witnesses or concrete proof. Otherwise, we will not be able to proceed with this complaint." With that he opened his desk drawer, dropped the ledger and pen in, and slammed the drawer shut.

Bendu held her hand toward him, palm up.

"What?" he asked.

"My pen."

Lieutenant Tarpeh opened his mouth to say something but then thought better of it. He grabbed the drawer handle and pulled. The handle came off in his hand and the drawer stayed stuck within the desk. Bendu and Agnes looked at each other and fought to suppress their urge to laugh.

"That's okay. Keep the pen," Agnes said as they hurried out and shut the door behind them.

"Sweetheart, darling, and love?" Bendu said, laughing. "My goodness!"

Agnes laughed too. "I'm glad you still have your sense of humor," she said. Then in a more somber tone: "You can see already—this is going to be tough."

"I should have been more prepared," Bendu confessed as they walked down the stairs of the Police Headquarters. "I mean, I just ran into Cobra this morning. I guess I was too anxious to get this done."

"That's understandable."

"Thanks for coming here with me Agnes. You know my own sister refused?"

"I've never met two sisters so different from each other," Agnes said, shaking her head. "How did that happen?"

Bendu laughed. "I don't know. We all wonder about that."

"She really made me vexed the other day."

"Don't feel bad yah, Agnes. She just doesn't understand."

"I know. She has a lot of adjusting to do in this new Liberia. She has you, though, so I'm sure she'll change."

Bendu laughed. "Siatta? I don't know. That would be a miracle!"

Agnes laughed too. "Well, let's come up with a plan to deal with Cobra first, then we'll help her."

"I just hope our time won't run out," Bendu said, serious again.

"Did he say how long he'll be in town?" Agnes asked.

"No, but he's at a hotel so we know it's temporary. He said he's here to take care of some business. That's all I know."

They walked out of the building and headed toward the Capitol Bypass in silence. When they reached the sidewalk to wait for a taxi, Agnes spoke again.

"Bendu, are you sure you want to pursue this?"

"Yes," she answered, nodding for emphasis.

"You know, you might be putting your life in danger."

Bendu thought about it for a moment, then looked her friend in the eye. "Well, that would be better than keeping my soul in prison."

Chapter 13

Moses Varney hung up the telephone and banged his hand on the table. "Damn!" he yelled. The last thing he needed was the police and Lord knows who else trailing him at a time when the need for secrecy was paramount. He got up and paced up and down the small hotel room. *Damn! Why did I talk to her?* He told himself he should have known Bendu Lewis would be trouble. She was trouble from the first day he saw her. *I should have shot her the minute she sucked her teeth at me!*

He opened the small icebox, took out a can of tonic, and mixed it with the last of the gin on the bedside table. He was pissed to think he literally handed her everything: his name, numbers, location. One of his comrades had called to tell him he was being hunted. What an embarrassment. He swallowed the gin and tonic down in one gulp. *That girl is smart. I should have known better. What was I thinking?*

His cell phone rang. He glanced at the number, cleared his throat and answered.

"Good afternoon, Chief."

"What's this I hear about someone trying to get the courts after you?"

Damn. "It won't happen sir. Our guys are in the right places. No one will let it happen."

"This doesn't look good, V."

"I can assure you sir —"

"You assured me you would be in and out of there and no one would know!"

"Things are under control sir. I promise you."

"Do you still have the goods with you?"

"Yes. I'm meeting Diallo in one hour."

"Make the deal quickly. We need to get a move on this thing."

"Yes sir, right away sir."

"And another thing: move out of El Meson right away. Lose this girl once and for all and get back to business."

Varney hung up the phone and began to throw things into his small suitcase. He knew moving was probably the wisest thing to do. He would go to The King's Castle instead of one of the more popular hotels. No one would track him down there. He would then arrange for the weapons to be rerouted, and he would head back north by the weekend.

Later that afternoon, Varney sped through the traffic in his Pajero, weaving between private cars and taxis like he was on a racetrack. There was no time to waste. He had to meet his airport contact and make the deal before the end of the day. A couple of drivers beeped their horns angrily at him, but he didn't have to worry about anyone stopping him for speeding. The police had no cars to chase him, and even if

they did have cars he would be ignored since he was using
a Senator's jeep, easily recognized by its SEN license plate.
Liberians joked that the letters stood for 'Since Elections...
Nothing!' They had one for the Representatives' cars too:
REP — 'Rebels Enjoying Power.' Varney chuckled at the
thought but then quickly sobered up and shook his head. *He*
certainly had some power, but what about all the foot soldiers
like his driver Weah? Weah had told him that as a combatant,
he finally had freedom from the constraining tribal customs
of his village, and hope for a decent future—that is, if God
would spare his life. Well, God had spared Weah's life, but
since elections...nothing, really.

Varney sighed and began looking for his landmark. He
had been directed to an apartment building in Sinkor. It
was a straight drive up Tubman Boulevard and then a right
turn on 9th Street, toward the Atlantic Ocean which was
just three blocks away. When he saw the building that had
been described to him, he came to a halt, jumped down
from the vehicle and quickly looked around the dilapidated
neighborhood to see if he had been followed or if there
were any suspicious-looking characters around. But there
were only several scraggly young boys and girls playing by
the building. They stopped what they were doing to stand
around and stare at him.

"I'm minding your car, chief," one boy said. It was no use
refusing. The boy would wait and beg for his fee anyway. Varney
smiled and nodded, remembering all too well his own life as a
scrawny, raggedy kid gawking in awe at "big shots" and never
dreaming that someday he would be one. He certainly never
wanted to be a big shot, and he often cursed the circumstances
that made him—at least on the outside—into that which he

so despised. The little boy grinned, and, taking his task seriously, drove the other kids back from the vehicle.

Varney instinctively scanned the space ahead of him as he made his way up the poorly ventilated, dark staircase with its moss-covered walls and mildew smell. His senses were honed to notice anything unusual, and he was listening intently as well. When he reached the third floor he knocked on the door and was let in by a short, fat man dressed in a suit and tie. Sunlight poured into the room through a large glassless window. There was nothing but a table and two chairs in the room. The table was covered with a clean white cloth. The man sat down and indicated with a wave of his hand that Varney should sit in the chair opposite him. Varney moved to his seat, and the man reached into the jacket of his suit coat, pulled out an eyeglass and a small piece of black velvet, and with a flourish, placed the velvet in the center of the table.

"Okay, put some ice in my Coca-Cola," he said, tapping on the black square.

Varney chuckled. He reached into his pocket and pulled out a piece of carefully folded paper. He opened it and spilled a small pile of rough diamonds onto the velvet. The stones shimmered in the light and Barry Diallo let out a slow whistle.

"Let's take a good look at these babies," he said, putting on his eyeglass. He began examining the gems one by one.

"*Beaucoup* USD right there," Varney said.

"They're beautiful."

"We want the next two shipments."

"No problem," Diallo assured him. "The first one will be on Thursday. You know you're getting *part* of the next two shipments, right?"

"Right, right."

"It would be impossible to explain the loss of *all* the weapons."

"The large truck we showed you will be enough?" Varney asked.

"Yes. Make sure the cover can be locked down."

Varney began to gather the diamonds.

Diallo reached over and touched his wrist lightly with his fingertips. "We need a deposit," Diallo said.

Varney kept on gathering the precious stones. "You get the diamonds when we get the goods. I thought they told you that."

"We changed our minds."

"But your guy is already down there with us. When we return to base with the truck, he gets —"

"I know the plan, but like I said, we changed our minds. What if he and his guards get 'lost' on the way back? What if you send diamonds we don't like? We can't risk it."

"And what if we give you a deposit and never see the arms?"

"You don't trust us, why should we trust you?" Diallo asked.

Varney glared at Diallo. "Look, I'm not authorized to make a deposit."

"Go talk to your people. Tell them we want half."

Varney stood up and stuffed the gems in his pocket. "You people are not serious!"

"A deposit. We're not being unreasonable."

"We have a deadline here!" Varney shouted.

"Then you'd better talk to your people quick," Diallo said as he put the velvet square and the eyeglass back in his pocket.

Varney reached the door in three strides and tried to open it, but it was locked. "Let me out," he demanded.

"I'll see you in a day or two," Barry Diallo said, smiling.

Varney scowled at him and banged on the door. "Let me out!"

Varney didn't have a 5 or a 10, so he gave the boy downstairs a crisp brown 20 LD note for minding his car. The boy became an instant hero in the eyes of the other children. They danced around him giggling and begging to hold the money too. Varney wound his window down and beckoned to the children. Still giggling, they ran over and looked up at him expectantly with wide, searching eyes, like hungry little baby birds in a nest. He took out a stack of bills and handed each child a 20 as they jumped and giggled with joy.

Varney sat in the Pajero for a moment, and looked up and down the streets around him through his tinted windows. Still no one. He started the vehicle and then looked up at the third floor balcony. Diallo was leaning against the railing, looking down at the Pajero while he talked on his cell phone. "Son-of-a-bitch," Varney muttered under his breath. He backed out of the driveway with a squeal of tires that both frightened and delighted the kids, then headed back to his new hotel to make some phone calls. There were a couple of people he had to take care of.

Chapter 14

Monday, Tuesday, and more closed doors later, Bendu started to wonder if maybe Agnes was right from the very beginning. Maybe this was going to be impossible. No one at the police station or in the courts wanted to help her arrest and prosecute Commander Cobra for war crimes. Maybe I should leave it in God's hands, she thought. Or in Calvin's, for that matter. One thing was certain: pursuing the case was already starting to take a toll on her work at Peace in Practice. She was behind on her proposal writing and follow-up, and that was not good at this crucial time in the center's history. With the fighting in the interior becoming more frequent, donors were getting timid about giving money to projects in Liberia and some international NGOs were even pulling out of the country. She and Agnes were both concerned that if PIP didn't get a new grant soon, they would have to scale down their major programs and maybe even go back to working from her home, as they did in the beginning.

On Wednesday morning, Bendu was dozing with her head down on her desk when Agnes's voice woke her with a start.

"Are you all right?" Agnes asked.

"Well, as you can see, I'm exhausted. Things aren't going too well."

"You need a lawyer," Agnes said, smiling like she just won the lottery. "Someone who can do all this running around for you."

"And why are you showing me your last jaw-bone teeth?"

"Because Calvin just sent one!"

Bendu gasped and broke out into a smile. "Calvin got me a lawyer?"

Agnes nodded. "From the best firm in town!"

That evening, Bendu took her first break from actively searching for someone who could get Varney arrested. She had tried all day to reach Calvin and thank him, but his phone was 'either switched off or out of coverage area' the recording kept telling her. She figured he was out of town or surely he would have called her back.

When the taxi stopped in front of her house, Bendu paid the driver and told him to keep the change. "Anytime, you hear?" he said to her, driving off with a big smile.

Bendu rang the bell outside the gate. When she didn't hear the familiar clanging of keys after a minute, she rang again, and this time the guard opened the gate right away.

For a second, Bendu thought she had come to the wrong house. She looked behind her quickly, and then back at the spectacular scene in front of her. A white palaver hut now stood in the middle of her front yard, with a freshly thatched roof, and an arch of tropical flowers in front of its entrance. She could smell their fragrance from where she was standing. Bendu moved a little closer. In the palaver hut was a small round table covered with a white tablecloth, and set for two. Over to the right end of the yard, a chef stood at a double charcoal grill tending something that sizzled and smelled delicious. But a movement on the left caught Bendu's eye and she turned to see Calvin Daniels step out from behind the bougainvillea, all dressed up and striding toward her with a devilish grin on his face. When he reached her, the subtle scent of his cologne made her knees buckle and he reached out to steady her.

"What are you doing in my yard?" Bendu asked, feigning disapproval. "Is this why you sent me these guards, so they could let you in anytime?"

Calvin laughed.

Bendu stared at the palaver hut again. "This is amazing."

"You need a nice break after all that's been happening."

"But this...and the lawyer!"

"You deserve it. May I?"

"May you what?"

"Sweep you off your feet!" And before she could protest he had her up and in his arms, and on the way to the house with her giggling all the way. As they neared the front door Bendu suddenly sobered up and asked to be set down.

"What's the matter?" Calvin asked.

"I need to get my keys out," she said.

"There's something else," he said, as he complied with her wishes.

"Carrying me over the threshold... I can't have that."

"Oh. Well, at least not yet."

"Calvin! You are getting way ahead of yourself, my friend."

He laughed heartily.

"In fact you can wait right here while I go wash my hands," she added.

"Hey, I need to wash my hands too!"

Bendu pointed to the water barrel placed strategically under the gutter. "There's some rain water for you."

"Oh, you girl! You're not easy o!"

"No, I'm not." And with a coy smile, she closed the door in his face.

"Hey! At least give me some soap!" he yelled through the closed door. But he found he was yelling in vain and would indeed have to make do with the water in the barrel outside.

Calvin had ordered dinner for two from Rhonda's Restaurant, a modest establishment with a reputation for having the best and most creative local food around. Rhonda Cooper herself had come earlier in the day to oversee the setting up of the temporary palaver hut and the kerosene torches that would provide romantic lighting.

Calvin helped Bendu get seated, then slid into the chair opposite her. They spent some time marveling at the feast spread before them by a smartly dressed waiter who seemed to appear out of nowhere. For starters, there was gingered plantain, grilled shrimp and chunks of onion still on the skewers, and sweet potato puffs fragrant with cloves, cinnamon, and nutmeg. The main courses that came later were Jollof Rice cooked with crisp pieces of cabbage, mixed vegetables, and succulent chicken; and a seafood mix of cassava fish, dried napleh, and shrimp still in their bright red shells all simmering in a pot of Groundpea Soup made with fresh roasted peanuts and served with fufu.

Bendu and Calvin ate heartily, and once, near the end of the meal, when their eyes met across the table, Bendu felt her heart beat a little faster.

Wait a minute, she thought. *This is all romantic and everything, but —*

Calvin smiled and raised his wine glass. "Let's have a toast."

Bendu raised her glass and clinked it against his.

"To the pursuit of justice," he said. "And to getting a date with the most beautiful woman in town—the one and only Bendu Marie Lewis."

Bendu smiled. "How is that article coming on?" she asked.

"My article?" Calvin laughed. "No, no, no. Don't try to change the subject. I want to spend this time getting to know you better. No talk about work, no talk about Moses Varney, no sadness, okay?"

"Okay, but you just asked me a million questions the other day. How about if *I* ask some questions this time?"

"Fine. Ask away."

Bendu looked at him and suddenly felt shy.

"Go ahead," Calvin said. "What do you want to know?"

"Tell me about my brother." She wasn't planning to say it; it just came out and she wanted to take it back when she saw the smile disappear from Calvin's face.

"Benji? What about Benji?"

Bendu shrugged. "He was so...happy. Always making a joke or laughing at something. That's what I remember."

Calvin smiled. "He was the funniest one among the boys in our class."

"Besides Daddy I thought he was the smartest person on earth. He had an answer for every question I asked."

"He loved you, Bendu," Calvin said quietly. "Though only twelve, he *really* loved you."

A tear rolled down Bendu's cheek.

"Hey! I thought we said no sadness," Calvin reminded her gently.

"Sorry. I've been thinking about him a lot lately."

Calvin sighed. "There's not a day that goes by that I don't think of him."

"What happened Calvin?" Bendu asked softly.

"What do you mean?"

"To Benji. What did you see?"

Calvin's eyes clouded over. "It was a long time ago, Bendu."

"Tell me."

Calvin shook his head and stared down at his food. "I don't remember."

"Look at me Calvin."

But when he did, there was something in his eyes that kept her from pressing the issue.

The two of them sat in silence for a while as the waiters cleared the dinner dishes and brought out a coconut pie and a watermelon basket filled with balls of melon and diced fruit in all their sweet, mixed juices.

Calvin spoke first. "You were in Duluma during the war."

"Yes."

"Tell me about it."

Bendu shrugged and thought for a moment. "I was captured by some fighters and...and kept there," she finally said.

"Doing what?"

"I was forced to be a rebel's wife," she said, without meeting his eye.

"How did you manage to get away?" he asked.

"He eventually abandoned me and after a while I just walked away from the camp."

Calvin held his fork in midair. "He 'abandoned' you?"

"Yes. He just got up one day, packed his things, left the house, and never came back."

She watched Calvin put his fork down, pie untasted. "But weren't you happy that he left? How can you say he *abandoned* you?"

"Yes, I was happy, in a way. But Samson was also supporting me."

"I don't understand," Calvin said, frowning.

"Well, that's how it was. I was forced to be with him, but we became like real partners in a way. He provided food. I cooked. He gave me protection, and he gave me a place to stay. Without him I was alone. Other men could bother me, I would have to beg people for food...all kinds of things."

"So you *liked* being with him? You *wanted* to be with him?"

"No, but in order to stay alive I *had* to be with him."

"Hhmm."

"Don't 'Hhmm' me. What are you trying to say?"

"Sorry, but it sounds like you wanted him—this rebel—to stay with you."

"No one knew how long the war would last. I had no clue whether I could get away, or what faction I would find just around the corner." *And I was in deep trouble*, Bendu thought. She looked into Calvin's eyes. They were slightly squinted. He wasn't understanding. How could she tell him any more?

She wanted to be honest with him, but if he accused her of *wanting* things to be the way they were, she knew she couldn't bear it.

"What's wrong?" Calvin asked.

His question snapped her out of her thoughts. "Oh, nothing."

"No, something."

"I guess you just had to be there to understand," she replied.

"Are you vexed with me?"

"No Calvin, I'm not vexed." *I just have some things to deal with, that's all,* Bendu thought. *And if you're not going to listen and attempt to understand, then what's the point?*

Calvin frowned. "There's something else going on inside your head," he insisted.

Bendu paused. "Actually, there *is* something I want to say."

"Go ahead."

"It's about the other day at your house. I was a bit disturbed by your attitude and some of the things you said."

Calvin thought about it a bit and shrugged. "Facts and opinions."

"Well —"

"Well what?"

Bendu sighed. "Nothing. Thanks for dinner. And thanks again for sending me Counselor Gray." She managed a bright smile. "This was a day of great surprises."

They made small talk while the waiters cleared everything away and packed their equipment into the restaurant van. Calvin asked the men to leave the kerosene torches until morning since the generator had not come on yet, but Bendu said she was tired and wanted to go inside and retire for the evening. She could see Calvin looked a little disappointed, but she *was* tired.

The waiters left with their torches just as the night watchman arrived. Bendu walked Calvin to the gate, thanked him again for a wonderful evening, and went inside to light some candles.

The first clue that something was not quite right was the strong breeze blowing into her bedroom from the broken window.

Chapter 15

Moses Varney watched Calvin drive away from Bendu's house. He glanced at his watch and told Weah to start the engine and turn the headlights on. It was 8:05 pm. The sidewalks were pretty clear at this time of night, and road traffic was scarce. To be on the safe side, though, they were parked in the shadows a good distance from the house, but close enough to see any movement outside.

"As soon as you see the gate opening you start moving, you hear?"

"I got it boss."

"I give her 10 minutes, maximum."

While they waited, Varney took a little plastic bag out of his pocket, scooped some of the white powder out of it with a long fingernail, and inhaled it through his nostrils.

Just as he predicted, Bendu's gates swung open less than ten minutes later. Varney slunk down lower in the back seat and Weah began cruising toward their target as the young woman raced out to the street with two frantic security guards right behind her.

"Bossman! The guards are with her!" Weah warned.

Varney reacted quickly. "Pass them, pass them! Drop me around the corner then come back alone."

Weah stopped when they were out of sight.

"Did she try to stop you?"

"Yes but she was also busy arguing with the guards," he replied.

"Go around quick, before another taxi takes her," Varney instructed as he got out of the car.

"What if the guards want to come with her?"

"Then you *don't* take them. I gotta tell you that? Just say you're not going that way and let them find someone else."

Weah pulled off and Varney began walking slowly. He could feel the weight of the pistol strapped around his ankle, hidden under his trousers. His heart was pumping fast, the adrenaline was flowing through his body, and thoughts raced through his mind. He wondered where she was planning to go running. To the police? Or to one of her friends? He had guessed correctly that she would be too shaken up to spend another moment in that house. He would get her and put an end to her meddling once and for all.

Varney heard a car coming and turned to look. It was not Weah. Damn. What was taking them so long? The private car went past him and disappeared into the darkness. There were a few table markets up ahead, lighted with candles. Varney didn't want to get that far. He didn't want anyone to see him get into the taxi when it came since the passenger, if she was alone, would probably cause a major scene. He turned around and headed in the direction from which he had come. This is not a good idea; she'll see me as soon as they come around the corner, Varney thought. "Oh well, what is she going to do?" he asked aloud. "Jump out and run?" He chuckled to himself. That cheeky girl was going to get what she deserved. He heard another car and saw the headlights coming. At last! It was Weah and there was only one passenger in the back seat. *Great!* He walked a little faster and Weah quickly pulled to a stop next to him.

Bendu started screaming as soon as she saw him. She reached over to lock the door, but Weah reached back, grabbed her by the shoulder, and pulled her away from the window and toward the floor of the car. Varney jumped in the back seat, held Bendu down by the throat with one hand, and reached under the front passenger seat for the blindfold and the duct tape with the other.

Weah drove off slowly, so as not to attract attention.

Varney was surprised at Bendu's strength. She was still screaming and struggling with all her might to free herself, even with his large hand tight around her throat.

"Shut up!" he growled at her.

Bendu's eyes were wide with fear and she continued struggling. Varney quickly covered her mouth with the duct tape, and ordered her to stay down. He took the gun out of its ankle strap, sat up, and pointed it at her.

"Do you have any idea of the kind of trouble you've got me in?" he asked, almost politely. She looked up at him, and now he saw a mixture of fear and loathing in her eyes. He raised his weapon and hit her in the head with it as he shouted with a rage that came from deep within his belly. "*Do you??*"

The crack of the gun on her skull echoed in the car. Blood streamed down from the wound just above her left ear, and she struggled to stay conscious.

Weah glanced at him in the rearview mirror anxiously. "Chief, you're going to kill her! *Take time o!*"

Varney reached up and pushed the man's head forward. "Keep your eyes on the road!" he ordered. "What business do you have telling me to be careful?"

Weah clenched his jaw and drove on, but couldn't help glancing back once or twice more.

Varney reached over and locked the door on Bendu's side, then put his gun under the seat so his hands would be free to cover her eyes with the blindfold and tie it tightly behind her head. She cried out with the pain of her injury, but the fight was gone and she sat still on the floor of the back seat.

Varney stared out of the window as they drove, and spoke without looking at her. "Because of you and your friends chasing me around town, my entire mission is getting messed up. I'm supposed to be preparing for a big to-do tomorrow night and here I am running after you to try and put an end to your ridiculous plan." Varney took out his cocaine again and snorted a little more.

Bendu sniffled and Varney looked down at her.

"What are you crying for?" he asked. "All your problems are about to come to an end."

Weah glanced at him again, bewildered, and the car dipped into a large pothole.

"Eyes on the road, damn it!" Varney yelled at him. They were heading uphill now, toward the beach behind Sophie's— or what *used* to be Sophie's. The once popular ice cream parlor was completely destroyed during the war and the yard was overgrown with weeds. The same was true of almost all the houses on this road, Varney noticed. And most of the area was in darkness. *Good.*

Not too long after the hill leveled out, they made a left turn and drove in silence for a little over half a mile before they turned toward the beach and parked facing the ocean. The moon lit up the black water and strong little waves pounded onto the shore. The tide was in, so the water came up almost all the way to the road that ran along the beach.

Varney got out of the taxi, sat on the hood of the car, and motioned for Weah to come and sit by him. He took a fat dujee out of his pocket, lit it, and inhaled deeply. After a few seconds he exhaled slowly and said, "I used to visit one of my friends who lived back here when I was a boy." He pointed to the huge black rocks in the water near the shore, just to the right of where they were sitting. "Just on the other side of that rock is a nice lagoon. We used to swim there."

He passed the joint to the driver, but the man shook his head.

"Since when you don't smoke?"

"I'm trying to stop, Bossman. That kind of smoking is not good."

Varney laughed. "What kind of smoking *is* good?"

"The war is over now, sir," Weah answered seriously. "I don't want to do bad things anymore. I just want to learn a trade or plant a farm somewhere and forget about this war business."

Varney nodded, but didn't say anything.

Weah turned to glance into the car.

"Don't worry about her," Varney said.

"It's quiet now Bossman, but people live back here and some of them are still up time like this. Maybe somebody will see us if you don't hurry."

"All right, bring her."

Weah hesitated at first, then opened the back door and pulled Bendu out. Her blindfold was soaked with blood. He led her stumbling toward the front of the car, and stood her up facing Varney. Varney ripped the duct tape off her mouth with one swift motion and pushed her down into the sand. She screamed at the top of her lungs and he lunged at her, grabbing her by the throat and covering her mouth with his hand. He looked around and noticed first one candle, then another flickering in the distance. *Damn! Had those lights been there before?* He searched for the discarded duct tape and saw that the sticky side was covered with sand. Useless. The girl was still wriggling, trying to escape his grasp. He pressed her close to him, tightened his grip on her mouth, and quickly forced her in the direction of the lagoon.

Chapter 16

Bendu struggled hard to get away from her abductor as he pushed her toward the water. The ocean breeze was cold and the salty droplets in the air stung the cuts on her head and face. She was grateful for this discomfort though, because it was keeping her awake and alert. She needed her wits about her. She wondered if Cobra was planning to drown her. Would he shoot her first? She hoped someone, somewhere in this dead of night, had heard her scream.

The roar of the waves was getting louder, and from time to time Bendu could feel the water come up around her ankles. Finally, Varney stopped. He made her sit down in the sand, facing the ocean. Bendu could hear him breathing hard, like he was out of shape.

"Don't you dare scream again," he warned.

He grabbed her hands and held them behind her back with one hand, while he untied her blindfold with the other. Bendu blinked rapidly and tried to look around as he tied her hands with the bloody cloth.

"And don't look back," Varney added.

Bendu kept her head still and looked around with her eyes as Varney tied the final knots. The beach was not easily identifiable, but she guessed they were in Sinkor or Congo Town. She was sitting in the sand and could see a huge black rock and a sort of lagoon on her left. A large ship appeared on the horizon and inched slowly toward the right, probably aiming to reach the Monrovia Freeport by morning.

Bendu heard Cobra strike a match, and the acrid smell of it tickled her nose. When she smelled the marijuana, she knew she was in deep trouble.

"My friends will be looking for me, Varney."

"I don't care about your friends."

"What do you want with me?"

Varney didn't answer.

Bendu felt him get up and move a little further away from her. Then she heard the click as he cocked his gun. She turned to look at him. He was sitting in the sand about six feet away from her. "*Six feet*," Bendu whispered to herself. "*Not a good sign.*" The taxi driver was standing on guard further up, near where the sand melded into the sparse vegetation and old, leaning coconut trees.

"Hey! I asked you not to turn around!" Varney yelled.

"Varney, please."

He pointed the gun at her. "Turn around!!"

Bendu turned back toward the ocean.

"I could kill you right now and throw you in the water. Or you could drop the charges tomorrow."

Bendu didn't reply.

"What will it be?"

Bendu actually weighed her choices. She knew he could kill her in cold blood, but could he see that he wouldn't get away with it?

Varney was losing patience. "Look. I don't have time for your games!" he shouted. "Answer me!"

"You messed up my whole life, Varney!" Bendu yelled back.

"What?" He sounded confused.

"You messed up —"

"What do you mean I messed up your whole life?" he interrupted indignantly. "What did I ever do to you?"

Bendu turned around to face him again. "You forgot?? You forgot you were the one who gave me to Samson?"

"I could have killed you! As far as I'm concerned I saved your life, only to have *you* come and spoil *mine*." He paused, and his voice was different when he spoke again. "Do you think you are the only one with nightmares?" he asked. "Please."

Bendu could hear his voice shake as he continued.

"Let me tell you, Miss Lewis. My nights are haunted by more demons than anyone can imagine." Now his hands were shaking too, and Bendu had to strain to hear him over the sound of the ocean.

"I didn't want to be there in the goddamn bush any more than you did," he said. "I studied business administration at LU. Wanted to be a labor lawyer someday. Not a damn fighter."

Bendu's eyes were still on him, and she physically felt her heart soften.

Varney wiped his face and looked at her. "*Not* a goddamn killer!" he yelled.

Bendu tensed up again. "Are you going to kill me now?"

"I want to," he answered, matter-of-factly. "The place where I am right now, I could kill you and nothing will come of it." He took a long drag on his joint, held it in, and then exhaled slowly. "What do you want from me? No one's innocent here. It was war-time. I gave you to one of my fighters, so what? You're still alive."

"And I should be happy?"

"You would rather be dead?"

"He abused me! Samson abused me!"

Varney shook his head. "I'm not responsible for that."

Bendu thought about it for a moment then she said "You know what? You're right Varney, but this thing I'm doing is not just for me."

"So now I'm symbolic of all that was wrong? I have to pay the price for everyone who died?"

"You haven't changed Varney. You're still using violence to get what you want."

"Violence comes in many forms, my friend."

"Understood. And if I could repent for everyone who hurt or oppressed you or anyone else, I would. But you killed innocent people, Varney."

Varney smiled wanly and took another long drag on his dujee while he stared out toward the horizon. "And so did you, Miss Lewis," he said quietly. "Or is your memory failing you?"

Bendu felt her eyes watering. "You made me do it."

"You could have refused."

"You would have killed me."

Varney looked at her. "Oh. So you killed to protect yourself? To save your own life?" He laughed sarcastically. "Welcome to war. War makes us *all* crazy."

He continued smoking for a while, and Bendu turned her back to him so that he couldn't see her face. She was confused and needed to think clearly for a bit, but the waves had been coming up closer and closer, and now a big one rushed toward her. She scrambled to get up and out of the way.

"Sit down!" Varney shouted. He strode toward her and pushed her back down into the sand. "Get up again and I'll shoot you." As soon as he moved back another wave came up and this time got her completely wet. She sunk a little bit in the sand and was pulled forward by the force of the water. The next wave was even stronger, and pulled her even further in. She looked back at Varney in a panic and saw that he had the gun pointed at her again.

"Did I kill someone you knew?" he shouted.

"You took my cousin Orlando, and you killed the person that I used to be," she shouted back.

"And you want to charge me for that, and for killing people who would just as easily have killed me and you?"

"They deserve justice. We all do. No justice, no peace."

Varney blinked rapidly, took one last drag on his dujee and tossed the butt onto the wet sand. "Can I press charges against you for what you did the day you left us?"

"I had no choice!"

"What are you talking about? We always have a choice!"

Before she could respond, another wave came up and hit her in the back, this time knocking her over and dragging her dangerously close to the water's edge.

"Let me get up, Varney, let me get up!" she shouted. "I'm going to drown!"

"Does your family know what you did? Does your writer friend know about your crime?" he shouted above the roar of the waves.

"Please..."

"Do they know?"

Varney stumbled and almost fell. He was so high now, he reminded Bendu of his worst days as Commander Cobra. "Do they know?" he asked again.

Bendu shook her head. "No."

"Will you drop the charges?" he asked. "Or will I have to tell them?"

Bendu struggled to pull herself further up the shore. It was hard with her hands tied behind her back. She could see the taxi driver looking on and pacing back and forth. Then he suddenly turned and disappeared behind the trees. Cobra turned to see what had made Bendu's eyes widen.

He turned back to her quickly. "Where is he? Where did he go?"

"Who?" Bendu asked.

"What do you mean 'who?' The driver!"

"You forgot? You shot him Cobra!" Bendu yelled. "You crazy dog!"

Cobra stumbled backward and grabbed his head in his hands. "No!" he shouted, reeling and dropping to his knees. "No!!" He looked at Bendu and then back to where he last saw Weah. He turned toward the ocean again, dug into his pocket and pulled out the little plastic bag half-full of white powder. He held it up to the sky, running and yelling in anguish as the breeze blew the cocaine away.

Bendu fell again and found herself almost completely immersed in about two and a half feet of water. She was in up to her neck and could see Varney had turned back and was rushing toward her. She went under and quickly worked to get her tied hands from behind her back and underneath her body. She stepped through them just as Varney reached her. He was so surprised when she suddenly stood up tall that he didn't even notice her hands were now in front of her, balled into fists. She quickly brought them up to his face and blinded him in both eyes with handfuls of coarse wet sand.

Varney dropped the gun and flung his arms about wildly, yelping with pain and trying to hit her even though he couldn't see. When that failed he ran in the direction of the retreating waves, knelt down in the water, and tried to wash the sand out of his eyes. The driver came back into Bendu's sight, zipping up his trousers as he ran toward her, and she knew she had to hurry. She crept up near Varney, braced herself for the pain she knew would course through her left hand, and with every ounce of strength she could muster, swung her tied hands to hit him in the most vulnerable place on his neck—just as she had been taught to do by his men at the Duluma training camp. Varney fell to the sand, unconscious, and she managed to pick up the gun just before the driver reached them. Bendu turned quickly and leveled the weapon at him, and he stopped in his tracks, holding both hands up in surrender.

"I beg you sister, *nothing's spoiled*," he pleaded.

"Move him up," Bendu ordered, her hand on the trigger. She stepped back and watched as the man dragged Varney up the beach and dropped him on the dry sand.

"Nothing's spoiled sister," he repeated nervously.

"Shut up," Bendu ordered. "You drove the car to bring me here then you say 'nothing's spoiled' between us?" She sucked her teeth loudly and told him to find something to cut the binding from around her wrists. She watched as he rummaged in Varney's pockets, found a small knife, and held it up so she could see it.

Bendu lowered the gun and moved forward quickly. The driver cut through the cloth that tied her hands together, and she breathed a sigh of relief. He put the knife in his back pocket and grinned.

"You see, Sis? Nothing's spoiled. Go before he wakes up."

Bendu hurried toward the road but halfway there she turned and motioned for the driver to come to her.

She held out her hand. "Give me the car keys."

The man handed them to her reluctantly. "Please don't take the car, I beg you."

"I'm not taking the car—just the keys," Bendu told him, glancing at Varney.

Avoiding the bushy shortcuts in case someone would mistake her for a thief, or in case she met a dead end, Bendu jogged steadily along the dusty road until she reached Tubman Boulevard. She stood paralyzed for several moments as she tried to remember whether there was a checkpoint between the Sophie's road and Calvin's house at this time of night, but her head was spinning and she couldn't think straight. She finally decided that it didn't really matter. Her fear of being caught by Moses Varney was greater than her dread of security checkpoints, and so she trudged on.

Chapter 17

Bendu's eye was almost swollen shut and the wound on the side of her head had bled so much that she almost lost consciousness twice before she reached Calvin's place. She banged on the metal gate and collapsed to the ground, exhausted. Through a narrow slit by the hinges, she could see the pinpoint of a dim flashlight zigzagging quickly toward her.

"Who's there?" the guard asked, opening a little peephole in the gate to peer outside. He couldn't see her but he must have recognized her voice because he opened the gate right away.

He was shocked to see her on the ground. "Oh, Sis! What happened to you so? " He helped her to her feet, rushed into his booth, and returned with a piece of paper and a pen, which he handed to her.

"What's this?"

"Visitor's Slip. You have to write your name, the date and time, and why you are here."

Bendu clutched the slip and almost choked laughing and crying at the same time. A light came on in the house and Calvin opened the door grumbling, but was shocked into momentary silence when he saw Bendu standing there with blood on her face and clothes.

"What the hell happened to you?" he finally managed to ask.

"Varney."

"Varney did this to you?" He grabbed her head and looked closely. "Where is he?"

"I don't know. I left him on the beach."

"Come in! What's so funny? I couldn't tell *what* was going on out here."

Bendu handed him the Visitor's Slip as they passed through the foyer on their way to the living room. When he saw it he flew into a rage and was about to go back outside and do Lord knows what to the guard, but Bendu stopped him.

"Oh, leave him alone Calvin. After everything I just went through I needed a good laugh."

"That one *was* a classic. Maybe I'll be able to laugh about it tomorrow. Hold on, I'll get a towel for your head." When he came back he was out of his bathrobe, and dressed in jeans and a T-shirt. He placed the towel on a pillow on the sofa, and had Bendu lie down on it.

"Which beach did you say you left him on?" he asked.

"Calvin, don't bother. He's probably gone by now."

Calvin stood upright and it was only then that Bendu noticed the gun tucked in the waistband of his pants.

Bendu sat up. "No Calvin, please!" she pleaded. "No more violence. Please."

Calvin started to say something, but then hesitated when he saw the fresh blood on the towel where Bendu's head had been.

"Let me see your head again," he said.

"He hit me with his gun."

Calvin peered at the wound. "We need to get you to Catholic Hospital. Where did this happen?"

"In the taxi."

"You got into a taxi with this man?"

"No. He got into a taxi with me."

"You can tell me about it in the car. And please, start at the beginning."

Calvin helped her up into his Land Cruiser and then climbed into the driver's seat. He put his gun in the glove compartment, and, at the gate, told the guard where they were going.

On the way to the hospital, Bendu told Calvin about the apparent break-in at her house, and the subsequent events. When she was done, he sat in silence for a moment.

"And you knocked him out on the beach behind Sophie's," he finally said.

"Yes."

He glanced over at her with a smile. "Out cold?"

Bendu smiled too. "Out cold."

"And apparently this taxi driver was a part of the whole plot. Did you get the license plate number?"

"There wasn't one, but I didn't notice until we were at the beach—when I remembered to look."

Calvin turned on to the short road leading to St. Joseph's Catholic Hospital. It was deserted at this time of night, and the hospital's generator—locked in a small concrete building to keep its noise down—hummed and whirred along with the crickets and other night insects that lived in the surrounding vegetation. Calvin drove through the gate and parked. As they walked toward the hospital entrance a nurse came out with a big bunch of keys jangling on a large metal ring.

"Wait!" Bendu exclaimed, reaching into her pocket. "I just remembered—I took their car keys so they couldn't chase me down the road!"

Calvin was amazed. "Good girl!" Then he gave her a puzzled look. "Why didn't you just take the car?"

"Stick."

"Oh. And why didn't you call someone when you found the broken window at your house?"

"The neighbor's generator hadn't come on yet so I couldn't charge my phone. Battery was completely dead."

Calvin shook his head. "I don't know whether to laugh or cry," he said seriously. "Listen, I'll call the police while the doctor sees you, okay? With the car in our possession we can identify the owner easily. You did well."

"Thanks. Please call Siatta too and tell her I need some clothes."

"How about your friend from work — Agatha?"

"You mean Agnes? No. No need to worry her." *Besides, she'll say I brought this on myself,* Bendu thought.

The gash on her head needed about seven stitches. While the nurse cleaned the area, the doctor wrote some notes in her file and then got the sutures ready. Bendu suddenly started to tremble.

The nurse patted her on the arm. "Don't worry. It will be over in less than one minute."

"Oh, I'm not scared of the stitches," Bendu said. "I just feel...faint all of a sudden." She swooned and held on to the desk to steady herself. She felt dizzy and nauseous. But she wasn't sure whether it had anything to do with the loss of blood. Varney was threatening to tell everyone about her "crime", as he called it, and she had to make a decision soon. The thought of disclosure was almost more frightening to her than facing Varney on the beach. If it had to happen though, she didn't want Varney to be the one to tell her story.

Dr. Wamah came over, held her chin, and looked closely into each eye. "When we're done here I want to have you admitted. We need to keep you under observation."

"I feel fine now, Dr. Wamah. It was just a spell."

"No, we need to keep you after such trauma to the head."

"For how long?"

"I can't say. At least a few hours."

Bendu sighed and thought if it was really going to be just a few hours, maybe she could make it to work by ten or so, after a little rest and some time to think.

Just after she was lying comfortably in a private room and hooked up to an IV drip, Siatta and Terrance arrived. Bendu heard her brother-in-law before she saw him.

"I'll throw that man in jail the minute we catch him," Terrance was saying in his booming voice as they approached her room with Calvin. When they got there Terrance stopped in the doorway, looked at Bendu, and thundered even louder. "How *dare* he do this to you? Does he know who you're related to?"

Siatta shot a disgusted look at her husband and ran over to her sister. They clung to each other tightly.

"You're coming to stay with us in Mamba Point," Siatta said. "The security we have up there is much better."

Bendu frowned.

"Don't argue," Siatta said. "It's the best thing. Your house isn't safe and you're in danger until Varney is caught."

"I have to get my work files and some clothes and things."

"Don't worry, we'll get them at some point," Calvin promised.

"How on earth did Varney know where you live?" Siatta asked.

"This is a small place," Bendu replied. "He could have just asked someone."

"Or followed you." Terrance suggested. "Don't worry," he added, "I have security forces at my disposal. We'll get him."

"That reminds me," said Calvin. "I need to go make another phone call."

Calvin walked out and Bendu watched Siatta and Terrance fretting over her. She wondered how they would react when she told them what she had done in Duluma and how she had left.

"What's the matter?" Siatta asked, seeing the pained look on Bendu's face.

"Maybe we should go and let you rest," Terrance said.

"No, stay, please. I want to talk to you guys."

Just then Calvin returned and the puzzled look on his face stopped her from going on. Terrance and Siatta turned to look at Calvin.

"What's wrong?" Terrance asked.

"Lieutenant Tarpeh. I called when we first got here to report what happened, and he sent someone behind Sophie's right away. Now he's telling me they couldn't find the taxi. His guys said the car wasn't there!"

Bendu frowned. "How can that be? It hasn't been that long since I left them."

"Maybe they had spare keys," Siatta said.

Calvin shook his head. "Maybe, but that would be pretty unusual."

"Wrong directions?" Bendu asked.

"No, Tarpeh understood exactly where it was."

"Well, maybe his boys didn't understand," Terrance said. "Those boys—you tell them left, and they'll go right. No sense sometimes."

Calvin frowned, unconvinced.

A nurse came in and checked Bendu's vital signs.

"Oh Bendu, didn't you want to say something?" Siatta asked.

Bendu shook her head. "No, it's all right."

"What was it?" Siatta pressed.

"Nothing." She looked at the nurse. "Actually, I want to know when I can get out of here."

"You really should get some rest," the nurse replied.

"But I'm feeling too restless," Bendu protested. "I'm just going to stay up until it's time to go to work."

"You're going to work looking like *that*?" Siatta asked, wide-eyed.

Bendu laughed at Siatta's reaction. "I can't afford to miss a day. Too much to do."

"I feel as though this is my fault," Calvin said.

"What do you mean?" Bendu asked.

"I left it up to you—this getting Varney business—when you refused to let me do it my way."

"Well, I feel if we want justice to prevail we have to obey the laws, that's all," Bendu said. "If those of us who know better break the laws, what can we say to others who do the same?"

Calvin smiled. "Do you really believe that, or is that a Peace in Practice lesson?"

"Both!" Bendu answered, making everyone laugh. "Plus, I really don't want to be a broken part of a broken system," she added quietly.

"And from what I've seen since I came home, it's a seriously broken system," Siatta remarked. "Probably broken beyond repair."

"No, there's always hope," Bendu said. "We can't go on like this forever."

"It's not always easy to be one of the few working parts in the system," said Calvin.

"No, but we have to start somewhere," Bendu answered.

Terrance smiled. "And what better place than 'with the man in the mirror', as the song goes."

"Yes Terrance, what better place?" his wife asked.

Terrance glanced at his watch, then looked at Bendu. "Well, Bendu, all I have to say is be careful. This man is dangerous."

"Do you think Varney would have killed you if you hadn't escaped?" Siatta asked.

Bendu shook her head slowly. "I don't know. The man was always unpredictable."

"What did he want?" Calvin asked.

"He wanted me to drop the charges."

"Then drop them!" Terrance said. "If that's what it'll take to get him off your back just drop the damn charges!"

Calvin raised his eyebrows and stepped back from the bed as if to avoid being hit by what was going to come out of Bendu's mouth. But she was calm in the face of this command to back down.

"No Terrance. I have to confess—I thought for one second about dropping the charges, but not to get him off my back. I'm the one on *his* back in this case, remember?"

"Why then?" Terrance asked.

"Because he threatened to reveal something about me."

"Something you did in Duluma?"

"Yes."

Siatta was alarmed. "Bendu! What did you do?"

Bendu swallowed hard and looked at each person sitting around her bed. Siatta. Terrance. Calvin.

My family and one of my oldest friends, she thought. Then she took a deep breath, and began to reach into the bottom of her soul.

Chapter 18

~~~

She was conscripted into the Women's Auxiliary soon after she arrived at the Duluma rebel camp, Bendu told Calvin and her family. The group had to train for combat just in case the men ever needed assistance at the battlefront. Every morning long before dawn, she woke up with the pepperbirds, drew water from the well, and swept around the house before she got dressed for drills. She hated wearing the uniform and the beret that identified her as a fighter, but she took consolation in the fact that she was gaining strength and learning how to defend and protect herself.

In those early months, on top of the physical punishment their drill instructor inflicted on them, Bendu said, Samson beat her for every little thing: his food wasn't ready, she didn't put enough pepper in the soup, the shirt he wanted to wear was not washed, his boots were not shined, she didn't answer quickly enough when he called her, his bath water wasn't hot enough, his bath water was too hot—was she trying to burn him? For some reason, if she wasn't in the house when he came home, that was the worst crime of all; twice he beat her for that within an inch of her life.

The violence was always worse when he was drunk or high on drugs. At those times though, he was also less likely to have sex with her so she stocked up on beer and palm wine. Sometimes, when her excuses didn't work, she gave him the liquor herself and risked the beatings.

The only bearable times at Duluma were the nights when Samson stayed in the bush fighting and didn't come home. On those nights she sat out by the fire "making fun" and listening to witchcraft stories with the other women who worked as rebel wives, fighters, and cooks. They ranged in age from about twelve to fifty, but were mostly young girls. She herself had just turned nineteen.

Among the women were Ma Musu's daughters, Hannah and Oretha. Though only fifteen and seventeen, they were also rebel wives. Hannah, the elder one, was a leader in the Women's Auxiliary and had the respect of all the men on the base because of her bravery and love for battle. After what had happened to her father, she *wanted* to fight and often went to the front voluntarily. Hannah was the "wife" of Joseph Davies, the fighter who had taken her to Cobra's quarters on her first morning at the camp. Many of the women wished they had been given to Joseph because he was so nice to his wife, but some laughed and said that with Hannah he had no choice but to be nice. Oretha, by contrast, was a sweet and gentle young woman who seemed to accept her plight and felt lucky to have her mother and sister there with her. Oretha's "husband" was a young general who was severely wounded during the fighting and had been sent to the main base for treatment, so she was alone and was able to spend a lot of time being a big sister and a teacher to all the little children at the camp.

Bendu managed to smile a little, now, when she talked about the women. All of them loved her, she said—the Congo girl who worked right alongside them drawing water, chopping wood, burning coal, washing clothes, and helping them write letters in search of missing loved ones. They felt sorry for her because Samson was one of the most notorious fighters around. Everyone feared him. He was usually drunk or high, and merciless to those he considered his enemies. Bendu told her family she had become somewhat of a hero, the way she hurt Samson's eye so badly during her first night with him. For days afterward Samson had to endure taunting from the other men and suppressed giggles from the happy women who gave her the war name Lieutenant TKO.

With help from the women in the camp, Bendu said, she had learned to live with Samson. Or around him, was more like it. The women served as look-outs and would tell her when he was coming so that she could get back in the house, look busy, and brace herself for whatever mood he might be in. To please his palate, they taught her how to make gaygba from cassava, and, to go with it, a slippery soup containing beneseed, bitterballs, and worlor dust—ingredients she got used to, but wouldn't touch now.

Bendu said she wasn't sure how Samson got money, but that for a while they always had food to eat, and she shared what was left over with her friends. In fact, all the women at Duluma base came to each other's aid in a way she had never seen before the war, or since. These strangers from different parts, thrown together by fate into a tense and uncertain situation, became family for each other in a fierce way, she explained.

Despite the new friends and the occasional fun times, the bad far outweighed the good in Duluma. As the war continued, food eventually became scarce, domestic violence was commonplace, and from time to time Commander Cobra and his men would discipline their fighters, gang rape women, and torture their prisoners of war right in the middle of the camp in the burned out concrete building that was known as The Oven. The screams of fear and agony were terrifying, and each episode would send the camp's civilians into a hushed and depressed existence for days.

In normal days—that is, before the war—the building served as both the school and the meeting hall for the village elders and other authorities, Bendu explained. But when Commander Cobra came, he and his men filled the hall with many of the villagers, locked the door, and burned them alive.

Bendu reached up and wiped a tear away. Thinking about the oven always made her think of her cousin Orlando—stripped, tabayed and taken off as a prisoner of war. For what? To fight? To be used for target practice? To carry heavy equipment when there were no vehicles? Sometimes not knowing was worse than knowing a horrible truth.

By the middle of her fourth month in the camp, Bendu went on, she began to suffer from dizziness and nausea. She was also extremely exhausted. One morning, after she fainted during combat training, she was excused and ordered to go and see Ma Musu, the resident traditional healer.

'Maybe I'm exercising too hard,' she had suggested to the woman. 'Or maybe it's something I ate.'

But Ma Musu sat in silence.

'Could it be the water?' she had asked, even though she always boiled her water.

'When was the last time you had your period?' Ma Musu had interrupted.

Bendu stopped talking at this point and tried to suppress her tears. Siatta hugged her and wept with her. Even Calvin and Terrance had tears in their eyes. Bendu swallowed hard. *I'm halfway there*, she thought, gathering strength from somewhere within herself. She wiped her eyes and went on with her story.

"My mind began to race and I kept shaking my head. *No, no, this can't be.*

I backed out of Ma Musu's room and ran to my own room as fast as I could. I kept going over my calendar again and again, counting days and trying to remember the facts of reproduction. I had marked the dates when Samson assaulted me, and there was no mistake: I was pregnant. Pregnant with a madman's child. The one thing I had feared the most had come to be."

Bendu shook her head as the memory of it came flooding back. "I felt like I had swallowed a poison that would spread and kill me if I didn't get it out."

For weeks Bendu had prayed for a miscarriage, and told no one else of her condition. She even resumed combat training drills—hoping that the strenuous activity would be too much for the baby to survive.

One day Ma Musu took her by the hands and said "My daughter, you are eight weeks along now. If you want me to take it out you don't have much time left." Lord knew she didn't want the child, but she feared an abortion even more. She decided to wait four more weeks and see.

At the end of the first trimester, the poison had spread and her secret was no longer a secret; her stomach was showing. She told her friends first, and then Samson, on a night when he was sober. He was incredibly angry—as if she had become pregnant on her own and on purpose. When he started to slap her and push her around she didn't even try to fight back. But her passivity didn't work. The baby stayed, and Samson became aloof and even more unpredictable. He didn't beat her as often, but when he did, it was severely. She was six months along when he suddenly deserted camp and left her totally dependent on the goodwill of her new friends.

After Samson left, Commander Cobra avoided her, but sent someone to tell her she would have to leave the house to make way for another high ranking rebel fighter. Against everyone's advice and despite their fears, Bendu ignored Cobra's order and stayed in Samson's place. As time for the birth grew near, she became stronger and stronger in her determination to take matters into her own hands and take back control of her life—the life that she had planned. And that life did not include a baby born of rape and out of wedlock.

Samson was gone, Bendu said, but she had new fears: fear of the birth itself, fear of needing a C-section and not being able to get one, of needing medication and not being able to get any, of getting an infection, of dying in childbirth. When the time came, labor was long and hard. The pain was like nothing she could have imagined. It was like nothing that anyone could have described. She was absolutely certain that she was going to die. She dealt with the physical pain by associating it with all the emotional and mental pain she had suffered. With each contraction she screamed with all the anger and rage and frustration she had been feeling since she got stuck behind the lines. With each push she visualized herself expelling not a baby, but a neatly wrapped bundle of pain and terror that she did not ever have to open and relive if she didn't want to.

Luckily there were no complications, Bendu went on, and the little girl who had kicked her for months, adding insult to injury, finally came out into the world. The women of Duluma somehow managed to find a tiny little blue and yellow dress in fairly good condition to present as a gift, but she was not in a mood to celebrate what she saw as the ultimate violation of her human rights and her freedom. She refused to nurse the baby girl during the two weeks that she had for recovery, and Ma Musu gave the task to a young woman who had just suffered a stillbirth. On the evening of the fourteenth day, Bendu had packed a bag of things and attached a note to it for Hannah and Oretha. Then she walked away from Duluma with nothing but pain in her heart and the clothes on her back, just as she had come.

Bendu closed her eyes when she had finished telling her story. It was dawn, and the pepperbirds were singing loudly in the plum tree outside the window of the hospital room. She looked at the faces around her. The secret was out. What were they thinking now? And Calvin...she couldn't read the look on his face. Would he desert her for abandoning her baby? What man would want a woman who could turn her back on her own child?

Over the years Bendu's thoughts drifted often to Baby Girl. Or "Bébé Geh", as everyone around her had pronounced it in their strong Liberian accents. She had not even bothered to give the child a proper name. If she was still alive—if she had not died of malaria or malnutrition or a bullet or a mortar attack—Baby Girl would be nine years old by now. *Nine and paying for the sins of her wicked father.*

Bendu said a silent prayer of thanks to God for people like Agnes who took in abandoned and lost children. *I, on the other hand, am just as bad as Tenneh's mother,* she thought.

No one in the room spoke for a while. Terrance fidgeted uncomfortably, and Siatta reached into her bag for some more tissue. Calvin suddenly stood up and stormed out of the room. They could hear him raging in the hallway, choked with emotion.

Part Two

Truth Lights the Way

Chapter 19

The offices at the Thomas & Reeves Law Firm took up an entire floor of the Maxwell Office Building. The waiting area alone was as large as the whole PIP office. It had a fresh new-carpet scent, and the air-conditioner had the place feeling like a crisp American autumn.

John Reeves was a good friend of Calvin, and had gladly assigned one of his junior attorneys, Counselor Marlon Gray, to Bendu's case *pro bono*. Bendu never would have been able to afford Thomas & Reeves, and, she thought, probably never would have found a lawyer willing to prosecute a former warlord. The attempt had been eye-opening, disturbing, and draining all at once. Why would no one rise to help her? How could so many people walk around so complacently, letting themselves be victimized all over again by the very same warlords, killers, and corrupt individuals who had brought the country to its knees? Calvin argued that the citizens voted for the leaders that they wanted, and so they couldn't complain. Bendu reminded him that some leaders had been appointed, and there was nothing they could do about it. Despite his general dislike of the government, Calvin also thought it was wrong for the people's choice for President to be shunned by the international community without being given a chance to prove himself. "You see? Democracy is only rewarded if the right candidate wins," he liked to point out. It was an endless debate that was taking place in many circles.

Bendu walked over to one of the large plate glass windows now, and could see the Executive Mansion, the Capitol Building, and the Temple of Justice clustered together in the distance. From up so high and afar the buildings looked so solid...so reassuring. They were symbols of civilization—of systems designed to work for the good of the people. From up so high and afar one could not see the crumbling walls or the crumbling psyches of the people within those walls. One could not see the writing on the Temple that said discriminatorily, "Let Justice Be Done To All Men."

Bendu felt Siatta's presence close by, and wondered what she was thinking of the view. Before she could turn to ask though, a secretary approached and ushered both of them into Counselor Gray's office—a beautifully furnished space with an impressive view of Monrovia and the Atlantic Ocean.

"At least now I can press real charges," Gray said, after he heard about Bendu's ordeal on the beach with Moses Varney.

Even Siatta was taken aback. "What do you mean *real* charges? What were the charges she wanted to press before? You didn't take them seriously?"

The lawyer struggled to redeem himself. "I mean *current* charges. More immediate. Easier to prove."

"Because if you don't believe I have a case you can just let me know now and I'll tell Reeves," Bendu added.

"Sorry," Gray said. "But realistically, until there's something like a Truth and Reconciliation Commission or a War Crimes Tribunal here in Liberia, it will be very hard to bring any warlord or ex-combatant to justice."

"I understand that, but let me tell you something," Bendu said. "Sometime during the war, I was in line with a big group of people, running away from one town to another. We had been walking for two days trying to escape from the rebels who were going around looting and killing near the area. As soon as we crossed the Johnsonville River we saw a checkpoint ahead of us. I felt a tight knot in my stomach as we got closer. Some of the people in line were actually crying already. Why? Because we never knew what to expect at checkpoints. Sometimes everyone would be waved by, but most of the time someone would be pulled out of line for a senseless death. Sometimes the fighters even made a game or a joke out of it. Sometimes they'd choose a pregnant woman and make a bet on whether she was carrying a boy or a girl—then they'd cut her open to see who won."

Gray fidgeted nervously. Like Siatta, he had not been back home for too long so he was still being bombarded with horrific war stories.

"You see how short my hair is?" Bendu asked. "It was halfway down my back but I cut it because I was tired of being noticed."

Gray fidgeted some more, and Siatta nodded slowly, as if she was beginning to understand something.

"That day," Bendu continued, "there were about a hundred and fifty of us walking together—men, women, children, and babies on their mothers' backs. Most of us had heavy loads on our heads. When we were almost at the barrier I felt relieved because there was only one fighter there, but terrified because he was a child soldier—the most dangerous kind of fighter. He had a gun, but he didn't look like he was on drugs so we had a bit of hope about getting through unharmed. He asked us where we were coming from. At first no one wanted to talk. Then one brave woman said 'Some of us are from so-so-and-so, and some of us are from so-so-and-so.' 'And where are you going?' the boy wanted to know. The woman said 'I don't know about everybody, but I'm going all the way to the border.' The boy said 'Oh, for true? Well, come. Let me help you get there faster.'"

Bendu paused, eyes far off in the distance. "Counselor, our hearts sank," she continued. "The people with the woman started crying quietly and the boy just stood there and waited. The woman stood still, trembling. When we looked, the boy picked up his gun and hollered 'I said get out of line and come here!' The woman started walking toward him, crying, stumbling, begging. When she had almost reached him he told her 'Stop right there; give me six feet.'"

Gray shifted in his seat and cleared his throat.

"You know what that meant?" Bendu asked him.

He shook his head slowly, eyes wide as if to say 'and please don't tell me.'

But Bendu went on. "Six feet away so her blood wouldn't splash on him. The boy leveled his gun at her, and the rest of us automatically backed up so that there was no one behind the woman. Yes, we knew the routine too well. Parents covered their children's eyes, and many people looked away, toward the rubber trees. One of the woman's relatives started crying loudly, and the child soldier looked at us. Everybody froze. 'Someone crying for this woman?' The crying stopped, and no one answered. Then he raised his gun again and shot the woman twice. No mercy, no reason. Then he waved us on and had the nerve—the nerve!—to tell us to be careful on the road. Someone picked up the things the woman had been carrying, and we left. It could have been any of us, Counselor Gray. *One man*, I was thinking. *One man, and one hundred and fifty of us. Why do we let them do it?*"

Siatta shook her head, speechless.

"Well, Counselor," Bendu said, "this time I'm stepping out of the crowd, out of the line, and I am taking action. I don't care how hard it is, or how foolish it seems."

Gray nodded again. "I'm sorry Miss Lewis," he said quietly. "Really. I'll do everything in my power to help you prosecute Moses Varney. But your best bet for getting him now, before he gets away, is to charge him for abducting and assaulting you last night. We'll catch him with the writ of arrest at El Meson in less than an hour."

Bendu nodded. "Fine, but just understand: this is not really about me and Moses Varney anymore. It's a lot bigger than that."

Chapter 20

Siatta's peaceful guest room, with its beautiful and calming blue décor, made Bendu feel like she was away on a much-needed vacation. She snuggled under the covers and closed her eyes for an afternoon nap. After all these years she felt she was finally on her journey to recovery. She had put off calling her parents, but would do so later that evening. At some point she wanted to talk to Calvin too. These would be the hardest conversations, but if they would forgive her—if they would still love her—then everything would be okay. She smiled at the thought of Calvin loving her, and he was the last thing on her mind before she drifted off and began to dream once more about her attempted escape from Duluma.

It was early in the morning, and she and some of the other women were scouting out a new place to gather firewood. The woods around the camp had already been stripped bare of all firewood and the skinny tree stumps served only as a reminder of what had been.

Away from the camp the air was sweet and clear and the sun shone brightly. Colorful birds flew and sang, and orange wildflowers swayed in the breeze. It was as if all was still well with Liberia, and with the world. She told the other women she was going into the bush to peepee; they should go ahead without her. Once the women were a safe distance ahead, she made her move in a direction where she thought she might find a new village and get some kind of help, maybe even transport to town.

The sun was unbearably hot, and she was hungry and thirsty. She looked back toward Duluma once or twice, but kept on walking; the taste of freedom was too sweet. From time to time another lone walker or a small group joined her on the same path. Some of them were angels who floated by, and among them she saw her Granny May and her beloved Jonah. There was a little boy too, who giggled and spun in circles as he floated past.

Soon, the sun was high in the sky. Another angel floated by, and Bendu recognized him as one of Cobra's men who went AWOL for three days before he returned on his own to face interrogation and death in the oven. She began to sweat, and although she was getting tired, a sudden rush of adrenaline got her walking faster and further away from Duluma.

As the sun began to sink, she finally came upon some signs that her journey was over. In the distance ahead of her she could see a small roadside market and a good number of people walking about. The village itself was back in a clearing in the woods, but she could see several wisps of smoke that told her it was indeed there.

As she approached the market, someone recognized her and started shouting 'Duluma spy! Duluma spy!' Soon, the whole village descended upon her. The more aggressive ones began to beat her, while the others looked on with interest or glee—as if the violence were entertainment.

Some of the onlookers started to chant: 'Kill her! Kill her!' But before the evil ones could tear her apart another angel appeared. A real one this time. It was an old man—the same poppay who had been left behind near Charlue Town and had told her God would bless her for not abandoning her grandmother. The poppay's word saved her from death, but the villagers began to escort her back to Duluma to face Cobra and Samson—a fate she considered worse than death.

Chapter 21

Moses Varney felt like a fool. Everything was going wrong, or had the potential to go wrong. Tonight was the night and he had to make sure nothing would spoil it. The operation had to be carried out smoothly. He would get the first shipment of arms, but then skip town and send someone else for the second. There was no way he could stay in Monrovia now. Not after what he had done to Bendu Lewis. Everyone would be looking for him, and he couldn't risk having the wrong people find out why he was in town. He opened up a hand-drawn map and sat down to study it, but his thoughts kept getting in the way: Why didn't he kill that girl? She practically said she would forgive him, but would pay no attention to his threats and would go on with the case. Why was she so driven to make him pay for what she had suffered so many years ago? Had she forgiven him or not? It was true what he had told her: His nights were haunted by more demons than anyone could imagine. Sometimes he felt he had paid enough. Even his daydreams were disturbed by the screams of women, the groans of men, the cries of babies, and, often, by the silence that followed once he had put them out of their misery. He remembered how the residents at Duluma avoided looking at him for days after some of his especially horrific actions. He would be striding through the camp, flanked by armed bodyguards, and see people hurrying by or darting out of sight, eyes always averted for fear that they would attract his attention and, logic followed, his wrath. Small children would run away, often crying, at the very sight of him. Sometimes he wanted to scream at everyone: *Look at me!! Look at me, goddamn it! I am a human being. A human being, like you!*

Back then, in the privacy of his room, in the darkest and the quietest hours of the night, he would sometimes break down and weep. The effort to weep quietly, when he really wanted to cry like a baby, caused his face and head to ache with an intensity that made him fear his skull was going to crack open. No one loved him. He was a monster. There were never any willing arms wrapped around his back. No soft gentle kisses. With the women there was only trembling, fear, crying and pleading. He put the lights out in their eyes, when every now and then all he wanted to do was make their eyes sparkle. With his reputation and a *nom de guerre* like Cobra, love was impossible and friendships were marred by distrust. Even the respect that men showed him came from fear. How did he perpetuate the belief that he would kill his own mother if she crossed him?

These days the only thing that kept the nightmares at bay was the self-induced stupor of drugs: marijuana usually, but sometimes cocaine or heroin when the pain was too unbearable and the guilt racked his body with sobs that threatened to choke him to death. On the outside he had to put up a front. Appear strong. Pretend he was still a vicious, deadly, dangerous cobra, ready to strike anyone at any time. Kill and not be killed. Inside he was struggling with a dichotomy of feelings: intense love for the common man, and seething rage at those among them who hated each other so much that they were blind to the possibility of progress for all. He was consumed with shame and disappointment at the disunity of his people and their utter failure to work together. Their downward spiral began as far back as the '70s, he was convinced, when wolves in sheep's clothing walked among them from the start. The 1980 coup was supposedly a success, but then dreams of redemption were dashed to the ground, plans unraveled, new repressive rules made to replace the old repressive rules, brotherhood betrayed, and compatriots executed at the slightest offense. What went wrong? Their road to redemption was that path from the little house on the beach where the coup was planned, to the Executive Mansion on the hill nearby, where President Tolbert was assassinated. The road to redemption—from the bottom of society to the pinnacle of power—apparently had too many unseen side streets and dark alleyways.

Varney sighed and concentrated on the map. No confusing highways to navigate, thank goodness, but he had to know where the checkpoints were, who was manning them, and which guys they would have to watch out for. The disloyalty of some people in Taylor's government was working for him now, but what did that really mean? It was no reason to rejoice; Dagoseh and other unscrupulous civil servants were giving them small arms and light weapons just for the money, not because they wanted a change of leaders that would in turn lead to a better life. Even if they got a better leader they would probably turn around and betray that leader too, if the price was right. No, there was no loyalty here, just as there wasn't any during the war. Back then, people were crossing lines and changing factions all the time—one day friendly with each other, the next day ready to kill. Today, there were quiet rumors that when the boys in the bush finally reached Monrovia they would chakla any plan that didn't give them "a chance to eat" like the big men.

Varney put his elbows on the table, closed his eyes, and rubbed his temples. Why did we end up killing our own people? Two hundred thousand dead! *What* were we thinking? He had asked himself these questions over and over again. Now he stood up, walked over to the mirror, and stared at himself. He had put on quite a bit of weight since he left the bush. His hair was definitely grayer too.

"What were you thinking V?" he asked himself aloud. "Why did you become so ruthless?" He let his mind hover over a possible answer—one he would never say aloud and didn't want to believe: *Maybe I wanted to be killed,* he thought. *Maybe I wanted to give this up long ago and let someone else lead the struggle for these apathetic people.* He shook his head. "They won't even stand up for you when you're rotting in jail for their rights," he muttered in disgust.

Varney opened the dresser drawer and looked at his gun lying there. He picked it up and examined himself in the mirror again. *Moses Varney with a gun. A weapon of destruction.* How did it come to this? After a moment, he put the gun down, and put his hand over his heart. He was having trouble feeling the beat, but he could clearly visualize the organ pumping blood. He had seen at least two hearts beat their last, right before they were ripped out of the chests of the legendary enemy fighters they belonged to and cut up to be shared among his men. Without warning, a nasty, bloody, rubbery taste rose in his mouth, and he rushed to the bathroom to spit. But he couldn't get the taste of the raw human heart out of his mouth. He suppressed the urge to vomit, walked back to the desk, folded the map, and put it in the inside pocket of his army vest.

He would go through with the mission, Varney decided, but he was beginning to have doubts about the strength and the future of the faction. Not that they couldn't win, but that they wouldn't do any better than the leaders they were trying to get out. What were they fighting for? Reconciliation? How and when would that come about with all the continuous killing and the displacement of innocent civilians? Democracy? That was laughable; they were trying to take down an elected president and were ignoring the cries of the people to let them decide his fate by the ballot rather than the bullet.

But he couldn't stop now; too many Congo boys were coming back home from the diaspora. Varney's heart burned with an old, familiar envy. Those Congo boys were prevailing, and seemed relatively unscathed by the war. You can loot their property but can't take their land, he thought. Can drive them into exile, but can't take what's in their heads...can't take that thing which keeps them standing. *What is it exactly?* he asked himself. *A superior education? A name? A history that began with survival of the fittest?*

Bendu had thrown him for a loop the night they met her on the side of the road. She spoke an indigenous language perfectly, and had given him hope—a little glimpse into the Liberia that could be. A Liberia where lines between classes would be blurred and where individuals would succeed based on what they know, rather than on who they know. There were definitely some Americo-Liberians—and there always had been—who were sympathetic to the cause of the people. Perhaps he and his comrades should have worked with them instead of being so distrustful and so fearful of losing leadership of the movement. If they had had the grace to acknowledge kindred spirits, would things be different now? Who knows?

Varney's mind went back to Bendu and he cursed himself again for ever stepping back into her life. He was sorry for what he did to her in Duluma, and he knew that eventually, for healing, all of them had to account for their actions. He just wasn't ready yet to face the music.

Varney looked at his watch. Three o'clock almost. Having stayed up the entire night, he had slept the morning away, confident that no one knew where to find him. He had five hours left before his *rendezvous* at the airport. Everything was ready for the meeting and the exchange. He was only expecting one final phone call from the chief to confirm everything. He considered going down to the bar to watch CNN or Sky News. Yes, that would be good. He could get something to eat and have a cold Club Beer or two to pass away the time. He looked at his watch again, wondering when the chief would call, and as if on cue, his cell phone rang.

"Where are you?"

"Hotel, sir."

"Listen to me carefully. There's a writ of arrest out for you."

Varney's heart sank.

"Assault and battery," the chief continued.

That bitch! He was right—but not only did she not drop the Duluma case, she had gone and pressed new charges!

"Get out now. No delays. Meet us at the Paynesville house." The chief sounded uncharacteristically calm in light of what was happening.

"And the mission?" Varney asked.

"Just get over here. You've got everyone scared to go through with it. How stupid can you be? You're supposed to be undercover and you attack someone? Then you let them *go?*"

Varney could now hear the underlying anger in the chief's voice. "Don't call it off chief. I have it all under control."

"This thing calls for discretion. You don't seem to have it." The coolness was back.

"Chief —"

"People are even wondering if you're still one hundred percent committed, V...if you can do what it takes to get the stuff to the base."

Varney cleared his throat. "Sir, you know I'm committed."

There was a pause on the other end. "Good. Then we'll see you in fifteen minutes," the chief said. "There's no time to waste. Don't even check out—just get over here now."

Chapter 22

Bendu tossed and turned in the throes of her nightmare.

The angry villagers were leading her back to Duluma. Back to Commander Cobra and Samson, and the dreaded oven. But then one by one the villagers disappeared, and soon she was walking alone. The sun became a dark orange ball and began to set in a sky turned lilac, with pink and blue streaks. The road began to incline, imperceptibly at first, then more and more until Bendu soon found herself climbing a mountain. The path was worn, and lined on both sides with wildflowers. Pretty butterflies fluttered among the petals and danced in pairs in the twilight. The sun did not set, but stayed suspended above the horizon with the sky changing into ever more brilliant hues. She reached the mountaintop and looked all around at the landscape below. It was beautiful. She was happy, and she was free.

When Bendu woke up she wanted to shout for joy. Her recurring nightmare had a different ending this time. It had become a freedom dream! She wanted to close her eyes and go back to the mountaintop, but she had a slight headache and was famished so she didn't try.

Bendu examined her stitches in the mirror and prayed that there wouldn't be a horrible scar left when they were taken out. She opened the curtains to look outside and was surprised to see that it was dusk. She had slept a long time. The full moon shone so brightly it lit up the crests of the waves of the Atlantic. "A full moon—no wonder it's been so crazy around here," she said aloud. The ocean was so close to the apartment that she could smell the fresh saltiness of it and hear the steady rolling of the waves and their gentle lapping upon the coarse golden sand. Bendu thought of her recent ordeal on the beach and had to admit, despite her initial objections, that she was glad to be in Mamba Point. If Varney or his guys could break into her house with guards on duty, if they could abduct her at will and torture her, she didn't want to return to her own place until he was locked up for good.

Bendu freshened up in the adjoining bathroom, then walked down the hallway, through a little sitting room, and past several more rooms, calling for Siatta and Terrance. No one answered. Finally, she reached the spacious living room and found her sister arranging the magazines under the coffee table.

"Siatta, your apartment is so large I always feel like I need a floor plan to get around!"

Siatta looked up. "Hey sleepyhead."

Bendu noticed her sister wasn't smiling. In fact she looked a little worried.

"What's the matter? Any news on Varney?"

Siatta shook her head. "Someone called Counselor Gray anonymously to say Varney had moved to King's Castle, but by the time the officers got there he had managed to dodge them somehow."

"How?"

"No one knows, but Gray just called from downstairs. Reeves sent him to give us an update and he's on his way up."

"I hope you and Terrance don't mind all this courthouse drama going on in your house."

Siatta smiled. "Of course not," she replied, as she went to answer the knock at the front door.

Counselor Gray looked very un-lawyer-like dressed in knee length shorts and a short-sleeved shirt, but had brought his nice leather briefcase along. He sat down and took out some papers while Siatta proceeded to pour them some drinks at the bar that took up a small corner of the living room.

"Who could have tipped Varney off about the writ of arrest?" Siatta asked from across the room. "Who knew besides us and the court?"

"That's the thing. Someone at the court could have some connection to Varney and his people, or any employee there could easily have been paid off," Gray answered.

"Aren't they supposed to uphold the law?" Siatta asked, coming over and placing small plates of hoummos, olives and Lebanese bread on the coffee table.

"Ideally, but integrity won't put food in their children's mouths," Bendu answered, reaching for an olive. "Government employees haven't been paid for seven months."

"One strange thing though," Gray said. "Varney hasn't checked out of the hotel, but all his things are gone. Looks like he skipped out without paying the bill. That's why we think he was running away to avoid the court officers who knew where to find him."

"Who called you with the tip?" Bendu asked.

"Oh, yes! He wouldn't leave his name but when I asked he said 'Don't worry, just tell my sister nothing's spoiled.'"

Bendu gasped.

"What? What does that mean?" Gray and Siatta asked in unison.

"It means 'no hard feelings'."

"Do you know who it might have been?" Counselor Gray asked.

"Maybe," Bendu answered, nodding.

"Are you going to tell us who?" Siatta asked.

Bendu smiled. "Well, it doesn't matter now, does it?"

"At least you have one of the bad guys on *your* side," Siatta said. Then she turned to Gray. "What if Varney left town?"

"Don't worry yet. Maybe he just moved to another hotel," Gray said.

"And how are we going to find him?" Bendu asked. "Go from hotel to hotel?"

Gray nodded. "If that's what it'll take."

"And what if he moved in with friends?"

"We just have to hope that didn't happen. He has business to take care of, you said, so he should be in town for a while —"

"Two weeks. We have to count from the time I saw him. And then I don't even know if that was his first day in town."

Counselor Gray was pensive. "Something's not quite right," he said. "We sent that writ the minute we found out where he was. The officers left right away, in one of our vehicles. I only called here to let you know it was happening. You were asleep Bendu, and Terrance didn't want to wake you."

"This is such a small city," Siatta said. "It probably took ten minutes for the officers to get from the court to King's Castle."

"Well, we've lost him. What's next Counselor?" Bendu asked.

"Your safety, for one. We should see if we can publish a restraining order in the newspaper so that he knows to stay away from you."

"Then what?"

"That's about all we can do at this point. Of course, we'll also continue to search for him. In the meantime, just be careful and try not to go back to your house."

"Don't worry, she's staying right here," Siatta said.

"But I refuse to be trapped in this apartment," Bendu informed them. "I'm going out whenever I want," she said to Siatta specifically, "injury and all."

After some more speculation over a second round of drinks, and an explanation of what the restraining order would say and could accomplish, Counselor Gray soon left. Bendu opened the sliding glass door to the balcony overlooking Sekou Touré Avenue. She and Siatta stepped out into the warm night and looked down at the few vehicles going by. The American Embassy was just around the curve and they could see a couple of their guards patrolling the street. There were several other luxury apartment buildings on this street, as well as the European Union and a few international NGOs. Médecins du Monde, Save the Children, and Action Contre la Faim were all a stone's throw away.

"All these humanitarian organizations here to help the poor and the displaced," Bendu said, "and day after day we've got Liberians somewhere creating more chaos, more Internally Displaced Persons."

"As you help one group another comes along," Siatta said.

"Exactly. At Peace in Practice we hardly have enough resources to help all the girls who are *already* traumatized. It's so discouraging sometimes."

The two stood in silence for a while.

"Hey, where's Terrance tonight?" Bendu asked.

Siatta shook her head. "I have no idea when he's going to show up. Let's go in; you need to call Mommie and Daddy."

"What's the time difference? I can never remember."

"It's either four or five hours. They're behind, so it's sometime in the afternoon for them."

Bendu sighed loudly, but didn't make a move to go indoors.

"Are you ready for this?" Siatta asked.

"Not for Mommie, but I just have to do it, that's all." She laughed and added, "I'm glad it's by phone and not in person."

Siatta wasn't so amused. "I can't believe you kept such a huge secret for so many years," she said.

"Well, as far as secrets go it was an easy one to keep. I mean, it tormented me inside, but I had no desire to share—believe me."

"How is Calvin taking it?"

"He hasn't talked to me since the hospital."

"Just give him some time. He really likes you, I can tell."

Bendu smiled, but didn't say anything.

"I just hope he doesn't bring the Liberian man nonsense to you," Siatta added.

Bendu raised her eyebrows. "The Liberian man nonsense?"

"You know what I'm talking about. The girlfriends on the side. Oh, and the secret children too." They laughed, but Bendu could hear something shaky in Siatta's laughter.

"Is that why Terrance isn't home?" she asked.

Siatta shrugged. "I don't know," she answered. "Things were fine when I first came home, then he started coming home from work later and later. Didn't even have the courtesy to call to say he would be late. Sometimes he comes home past midnight, smelling like cheap perfume or like he's been laying down in some hooker's hovel somewhere."

"What does he say?"

"I don't ask questions. He gives no excuses, no explanation, nothing. He just comes home and gets into bed as if this is a normal thing to do."

"At least he doesn't lie to you. That would make it worse."

"He's been very elusive lately, though. Something's going on but I can't figure out what it is."

"Are you just going to let the affairs go on? Have the two of you talked about it?"

"Once he had the nerve to tell me he was 'keeping company' with other women because I wasn't sleeping with him. What he conveniently forgot was that I'm not sleeping with him *because* he's sleeping around."

"So that's how you're dealing with it?"

"This is my *life* we're talking about," Siatta pointed out. "We live in sub-Saharan Africa with HIV everywhere and almost no access to anti-retroviral drugs. I refuse to die of AIDS."

"He's not careful?"

"How should I know what they do? I just need to protect myself."

They both looked out over the balcony in silence, and Bendu thought about Siatta's grand wedding with all its promises of happily ever after. Siatta was so beautiful that day, and Terrance Clarke…well, he was the picture of a knight in shining armor. Prince Charming in the flesh. Who would have thought?

Siatta smiled wistfully at Bendu. "He was a regular Prince Charming, wasn't he?" she asked, as if Bendu had expressed her thoughts aloud.

Bendu felt goose bumps rise on her arms and reached out to hold Siatta's hand. It had been a long time since they shared such sisterly magic.

"You know, Terrance is a very well-educated man but he really believes he can tell whether a girl is HIV-positive or not just by looking at her," Siatta said.

Bendu was aghast. "No!"

"Yes o. To him a pretty girl can't possibly be infected."

"Doesn't he read?"

"Even if he couldn't read, the fact that he got a sexually transmitted infection from one of those girls should tell him something."

"My goodness."

Siatta chuckled. "I guess we all have our secrets," she said. "Speaking of which, you'd better go back inside and make that call."

As it turned out, Eva Lewis was not the parent to be worried about. Bendu's father was the difficult one. He had no comment about what had happened to her in Duluma or about how she had left her baby. Bendu figured he was probably just too hurt or shocked by the news and needed a little more time to sort out his feelings. Eva, on the other hand, was bursting with questions and excitement about her "grandchild".

Grandchild.

Bendu mulled over the word later on, and realized she had never thought about the connections before. Baby Girl was not just hers. Not only a daughter. *A daughter!* No, she was also a niece and a grandchild. She was *theirs*...and she was lost.

Chapter 23

Bendu went to work on Monday afternoon and, in the PIP foyer, paused longer than usual at the photograph of Liberian women with their sisters from Guinea and Sierra Leone marching for peace. She had spent the morning at a meeting of humanitarian organizations and was returning with bad news: USAID funding was decreasing once again, and the European Union would continue giving funds for emergency and rehabilitation, but still nothing for development. The Carter Center was leaving, and so were two international NGOs. Worst of all, the main proposal she and Agnes had been counting on had been rejected by the organization to which they had submitted it. It was a good proposal, but the NGO was no longer sure of getting more funds to work with national partners like Peace in Practice.

Bendu looked at the women in the photograph, all dressed in black and white. "Black to symbolize our grief, and White to symbolize our hope," they had declared. But one year later, and the war still waged on in rural Liberia. *Hope. I've got to keep hope alive,* Bendu reminded herself.

Bendu walked into PIP's weekly group counseling session not knowing how she would be able to stay focused. But she didn't have an opportunity to let her mind drift. Josephine and Rosetta were extremely excited to see her, and all of them were surprised a minute later when Tenneh came with the news that she did not have TB as everyone had suspected, but an infection which, although serious, was not contagious.

The girls had a barrage of questions for Bendu. Agnes tried to bring some order to the session, but the girls had not seen Bendu since the attack by Moses Varney, and they could not be contained.

"You see what he did to you?" Rosetta said. "These fighters don't change. See how wicked they are?"

"We want to know the whole story—from the first time you saw him," Josephine pleaded.

"That's a real *Titanic* you're asking for, Josephine," Rosetta said. "We'll be here all day."

Bendu smiled at the slang reference to the extra long movie. "The first thing I have to do is make a confession," she told them. "Even after all the role plays we've done in this room and after all the counseling and advice I've given, I was in complete shock when I actually had to face this situation."

"Can you tell us about some of the things you learned?" Agnes asked.

"Well, first of all, you can't change what happened in the past, but you *can* control the way you respond. Remember what we always said during the war? *'What doesn't kill me...'* "

"Will only make me stronger!" the girls finished in unison.

"That's right," Bendu said. "You have to decide to emerge stronger from whatever you experience. On the practical side, when you come face to face with your past—literally, like I did—you need to assess the situation quickly. Is there need for alarm? What are your choices? Should you confront the perpetrator, or just walk away? What will give you closure?"

"In other words," Agnes explained to the girls, "ask yourself what has to happen to let the *palaver* be finished."

Rosetta raised her hand. "Does forgiving someone mean letting them get away with what they did?"

"I'm still struggling with that question myself," Bendu admitted. "It helps to remember the context in which the offense happened."

"In other words," Agnes explained again, "you need to think about what was happening around you at the time. Why did the person harm you? Did he really have something against you, or was his behavior expected or forced by others above him?"

Rosetta pushed out her full lips. "Nobody's forced to do anything."

"I hear what you're saying," Josephine said, "but now we have to stop and ask ourselves this question: *Even though violence was done to me, how will I practice peace?*"

"Exactly!" Agnes said.

"But that means you mustn't try to get revenge," said Rosetta, sounding a little disappointed.

"Well is it really revenge we want?" Bendu asked. "Or is it justice? In *my* case I see that peace for me will only come if there is some form of justice."

Agnes addressed the group again. "How many of you remember during the war asking 'Mama why are they carrying that man away?' or 'Why are they beating that person?'"

Each girl raised her hand and nodded. They remembered too well.

"And what did the people around you say?" Agnes asked.

"Don't ask questions," Josephine answered.

Tenneh raised her hand. "Don't talk about these things. Just let it go."

"If you open your mouth, they will carry you too," Rosetta said quietly.

"And did any of you ever try to help those people anyway?" Agnes asked.

The girls shook their heads.

"So you see, some of us are guilty of committing atrocities and some of us are guilty of doing nothing," Agnes said.

Bendu looked at Agnes and wondered for a moment if she was trying to accuse her of something. But Josephine's next question brought her back to the moment.

"What was the hardest thing about seeing that man?" Josephine asked.

"He knows things about my past that I never told anyone," Bendu answered. "When I saw him here in town I started thinking more about everything I had been trying to forget and to hide." Her voice became quieter as she continued. "I had a baby during the war. Her father was a rebel, and when she was born I … I left her and ran away from the camp."

"Ay yah, for true?" Rosetta couldn't believe it.

"Yes o, that's what she did," Agnes said.

Bendu ignored Agnes and went on speaking. "I told my family about it when I was in the hospital, and now that it's all out I feel like a big burden has been lifted off my shoulders. You know, Sis Agnes always tells us 'you can't let the past rule your future' but that's just what I was doing. The secrets were really affecting my life."

Tenneh, who had been quieter than usual, finally spoke up. "Sis Bendu, you've really encouraged me," she said. "Telling your secret is not only helping you—it's helping other people too." She cleared her throat and went on. "That's why I want to tell all of you something."

The other girls and the counselors looked at her expectantly.

"Well, you know how I'm quick to get sick. I've been going to the hospital for malaria, for coughing, for all kinds of things. Well, this last time they tested me for HIV."

"The test was positive?" Agnes asked.

Tenneh nodded.

Bendu's heart sank, and she could find no words to say immediately.

"So you've got AIDS?" Rosetta wanted to know.

"Well, I have the virus that causes AIDS. The doctor thinks I've had it for a long time and it's just recently that my immune system is starting to get weak."

Rosetta frowned. "So you'll just keep getting sick?" she asked.

"I'm supposed to try to keep myself up by eating well," Tenneh answered, "but where will I get money to eat well? Even trying to pay my way to come to class is hard sometimes."

"And there's no cure," Josephine said sadly.

"Well, there's no cure but there's medicine that helps keep the virus down," Tenneh said. "The HIV and AIDS counselor at the hospital told me if more HIV-positive people are willing to talk about having HIV, we could help others learn how not to get the virus. We could even help governments do more for people living with HIV or AIDS."

"You're right, Tenneh," Bendu said softly. "I'm so sorry this happened to you. How are you feeling?"

"I feel alright now, but sometimes my whole body feels weak."

"Are you scared?" Josephine asked.

"Yes, but I'm not scared of dying. I'm only scared of how people will act if they find out."

The girls nodded and Bendu wondered how they could all help Tenneh thrive in spite of the virus.

"What do you think people will do?" Agnes asked Tenneh.

"Well, all of us here had the HIV and AIDS workshop together, so we know you can't get HIV from someone just by being friendly with them," Tenneh answered. "But many people don't know that. I'm afraid that people will run away from me, or even try to harm me."

"Don't worry about that," Josephine said. "No *chéchépolay* will leave this room. We won't tell anybody."

"But you know what? I'm not worried about you gossiping at all," Tenneh told them. "I don't want to keep this a secret. I want to do what Sis Bendu's doing. If my story can help somebody else, even *one* person, I will tell it."

Wow, Bendu thought. *Here I am trying to figure out how we can help her, and she already has a plan to help the nation!*

The counseling session continued with the topic of the day, and no one treated Tenneh any differently. The young girl seemed happy and at peace. The energy in the room was almost tangible, and Bendu was pleased to see how effective their HIV and AIDS awareness training had been. *This is our way out*, she thought. *Openness, acceptance and healing—one person at a time.*

Chapter 24

Bendu and Agnes straightened up the empty counseling room in uncharacteristic silence. Bendu was preoccupied by what had just transpired there: Tenneh with HIV, her own wavering convictions about Varney, and Miss Agnes acting holier than thou. What was happening?

"You need to forgive him," Agnes said suddenly.

Bendu spun around. "What did you say?"

"Commander Cobra. Moses Varney. You need to forgive him once and for all."

"Please don't tell me what to do."

"I'm only trying to help you."

Bendu sighed. "Sorry, I didn't mean to be so —"

Agnes smiled. "It's all right. I knew that's what you were going to say."

"In fact, that's one of the main things on my mind, Agnes," Bendu said. "You know, there were moments on the beach when I saw Cobra in a different light. I wanted to let it all go, but..."

Agnes sat down and indicated that Bendu should sit in the chair facing her. "But what?"

"Well, one minute he would seem sorry, then the next minute he would say or do something else and I would change my mind."

"Are you thinking of dropping the charges?"

"No, not at all."

"I think you're giving the girls a mixed message, Bendu. We teach them that repentance and forgiveness is the way to fix the relationships we've destroyed, but then you come by..." Agnes let her voice trail off.

"But then I come by and what? Show them that it's not an easy thing to do? Well it *isn't* an easy thing to do! And you know what? I did not appreciate you saying that whoever is without sin should throw the first stone."

"I did *not* say that!"

"Well you implied it, and *you* haven't exactly repented for what you did during the war so get off my case."

Agnes didn't respond, and the two sat in silence for a while.

In a calmer voice, Bendu tried to explain. "It's not that I don't want to forgive him. I just don't want to be a disappointment to other girls or the victims who can no longer speak up. I feel like I'm doing this for them too. Forgiving seems like taking the easy way out. Like I would no longer be struggling for justice."

Agnes sighed. "Not at all, Bendu. I think maybe you've just grown enough to see things from a different angle. It's harder to forgive than to punish. In some cases it's wiser too, and better for everyone in the long run."

"It would be easier if he had changed from his old ways," Bendu argued. "You know, some people were forced into violence and did what they had to do to survive. Others are just plain evil in their hearts and act the same in war *or* peace."

"True, but who's to say which category someone falls into?" Agnes wanted to know. "It's not always clear. Do we just punish everybody who hurt someone? Do we even punish the people who were only trying to protect themselves?"

Bendu sighed. This was another never-ending debate.

"Do you think Cobra is an evil person?" Agnes asked.

"Well look what he just did to me."

Agnes laughed. "You were spoiling his plans."

Bendu wasn't amused. "There's no excuse for violence," she said.

"You're right," Agnes said, "but here's the thing: Happiness comes from making other people happy, certainly not from trying to make a particular person *un*happy. All this energy you've been using to pursue Cobra could be put toward something else."

Bendu didn't say anything.

"I'm going to give you an assignment."

"Oh no," Bendu said, eyeing her friend suspiciously. "What is it?"

"The same one the girls did. Write a letter to Commander Cobra, or to Samson, or whoever you feel you need to talk to. It will help you sort out your feelings."

Bendu nodded. "You might be right, Agnes. I'll try it."

As Bendu got up to leave, Agnes stopped her. "Please wait small."

"What is it?"

Agnes averted her eyes and smiled shyly.

"Go ahead, tell me what you're thinking," Bendu said, sitting down again.

"I don't know what you'll think of this," Agnes said, "but I have an idea."

Bendu smiled. "Ideas are good," she encouraged.

"The letters we have the girls write set me thinking—maybe we could start a Truth Project here at the Center."

"How would it work?"

"First, we would invite survivors of violence—both victims and perpetrators—to come in and talk about their experiences in the midst of a group of counselors and community leaders," Agnes began. "We would open it up to anyone who wants to come. It would give people a chance to tell what happened to them, or to explain why they did certain things and ask for forgiveness."

"Now, would these 'perpetrators' be asking forgiveness directly from the person they —"

"Oh, no," Agnes interrupted. "But if such a case came up and both parties involved want to, we could arrange something. The main goal of this project would be to help people start healing by opening up."

Bendu listened intently, and even before Agnes had finished describing all the other components of her proposed program, she knew the Truth Project was something they had to implement at Peace in Practice.

By the end of the day, exhausted from trying to sort out everything on her mind and in her heart, Bendu was eager to get home. She left Agnes still working, and headed to her temporary home in Mamba Point. She didn't have a spare key yet, but Siatta was there to let her in.

As soon as Bendu stepped inside she noticed the dining room table was adorned with a stunning bouquet.

"Gorgeous flowers!" she exclaimed. "Where did you get them? Terrance repenting?"

Siatta smiled. "They came from Terravilla Gardens, and they're yours."

Bendu's mouth fell open. She went toward the table and read the note attached to one of the long stems: *Sweet Bendu, Hope you are feeling better. Love Always, Calvin.* She looked at Siatta and smiled. "Calvin," she said softly.

"He called to see if they had arrived," Siatta told her. "He said he ran off because he needed some time to 'deal with his own demons,' whatever *that* means."

Siatta plopped down on the sofa with her magazines while Bendu, in awesome wonder, admired the striking blossoms that only an amazing God could have made.

"Calvin's always been intense," Bendu said, smiling.

"He used to be so in love with you when we were kids. How come you two never got together?" Siatta asked.

Bendu laughed. "Well, he was Benji's friend and they were always together. I guess I just saw him as another brother—even after Benji died."

Siatta sighed. "Yeah, I see how that could happen," she said.

Bendu looked over at her sister and saw a wistful look in her eyes. "When did Terrance come home last night?" she asked quietly.

"Who knows? I went to bed right after you did and didn't wake up until this morning. I guess he snuck in quietly so I wouldn't hear him." She chuckled.

"I don't know how you can laugh about what he's doing to you."

"Well, sometimes we laugh to keep from crying. That's what you always tell me when I ask why Liberians laugh when they tell their terrible war stories. Anyway, *I* don't know how you can keep pressing this Cobra issue."

"Actually, I've been thinking about it all day," Bendu said. "I still think Moses Varney is dangerous, but the bitterness toward him is gone and I want to move on. I'll still let the lawyer pursue him, but until he's found I want to put *my* energy toward finding my daughter."

Siatta frowned "Bendu! What if she's —"

"Dead? I've thought about that. But what if she's not?"

"What if she doesn't want to see you?"

"I've thought about that too," Bendu answered, as she headed to her room to put her things down and take off her shoes.

"You're crazy!" Siatta called out affectionately.

Bendu smiled to herself. Siatta was right. She was already overwhelmed by everything that was happening in her life: Commander Cobra, the assault, working with lawyers, being temporarily displaced, falling in love with Calvin, funding challenges at work...and now she was going to add one more thing. It would probably be like looking for a needle in a haystack, but she was going to try her best to find Baby Girl. She would start by visiting ICRC—the International Committee of the Red Cross. They had a message system she could use to try to reach Ma Musu, Hannah and Oretha, wherever they were, in the hope that they would be able to give her news about Baby Girl. What if the child *was* alive? What were *her* torments? Sometimes pain only increased with time, and too much time had passed already. Now it was time to make amends.

Chapter 25

On Tuesday morning, Bendu got out of the car in front of the ICRC office on Bushrod Island, and took a moment to study the mural on the white fence enclosing the compound. The large painting showed armed men forcing villagers to leave their homes. Two of the armed men were snatching property from some of the terrified people, and the caption underneath begged fighters to respect the rights of civilians. *A scene played out in civil wars all across Africa*, Bendu thought. *Twelve years of terror in Liberia! When will it ever end?*

The uniformed security guard at the ICRC gate made a phone call to announce Bendu's visit, then gave her a badge with a number on it and asked her to sign the visitor's log. He gave her directions to the tracing office and she thanked him. *I can't believe I'm doing this!* she thought, walking down the long hallway and wishing she had brought Agnes or Siatta along for support. .

The tracing assistant was a young man with an encouraging smile that immediately put Bendu at ease. He introduced himself as Gabriel, and invited her to sit down. Bendu glanced around the office while he searched for the forms she needed. There were about eight large file cabinets lined up against two of the walls. The labels on the drawers told her they contained files from Guinea, Sierra Leone, Liberia, Ghana, Côte d'Ivoire and Nigeria. Bendu sat in solemn thought. *All those missing children! Hundreds and hundreds of them.*

When Gabriel handed her the tracing request form, Bendu looked at it and blinked back tears.

"What's the matter?"

"My daughter. The first thing you ask for is her name."

Gabriel looked puzzled. "Well, yes."

"I don't even know her name. We only called her Baby Girl."

"That's okay; there's a space on the form for a nickname," Gabriel said. "How old was she when you were separated from her?"

"Two weeks."

"Oh, a young baby! And this was in what year?"

"1992."

"How come you waited so long to try and find her?"

Bendu shook her head. "The war...everything...I guess I almost didn't believe she could still be alive."

"So what made you come in today?" he asked gently.

"I want to try," Bendu answered quietly. "Just in case she's one of those children in your files."

There was a moment of silence and Gabriel looked a little worried. "Nine years is a long time o," he finally said.

"That's true," Bendu agreed, "but I think I know who might be able to tell us what happened to her."

The tracing assistant smiled. "Good. Then we have a place to start," he said. "I suggest you send a Red Cross message to try to reach the person who might have your child or know her whereabouts. Fill out a tracing request too, even if you have to leave some spaces blank, and we'll put what you have in the computerized database. It might turn out to be useful. You never know."

The tracing request form was extensive, and included pertinent questions such as date of birth, tribe, parents' names, place of separation, and cause of separation. Bendu decided to write three Red Cross messages in case Ma Musu and her daughters were no longer all together. Any one of them would be able to lead her in the right direction. When she was finished, she asked Gabriel about the next steps in the process. He told her they would start by searching the databases for Baby Girl in case she had been registered at some point. The messages would be sent to the ICRC animators in the camps where the women may have moved to after they left Duluma. Members of the same tribe tended to travel and settle together, Gabriel explained. The animators would follow leads and keep on searching, and would give the Monrovia office an update every two months.

"So should I call you every two months to check?" Bendu asked.

"No, we'll get in touch with you," Gabriel told her. "We usually send a caseworker to the home, but if you have a cell phone we'll be glad to call."

Bendu sighed. "So now I just wait?"

"That's right."

"It's been almost ten years, but I don't know if I can wait another ten *minutes!*"

Gabriel laughed. "Don't worry," he said kindly. "If it's meant to happen, it will."

As Bendu left the ICRC office, she prayed that Ma Musu or Hannah or Oretha had registered Baby Girl as a separated child after their escape from Duluma. But what if they had decided to just keep her as their own? What if Baby Girl wasn't registered and the women couldn't be found? Bendu thought of the unaccompanied child that Agnes had found and raised. Agnes loved that boy dearly, but what if he had a mother somewhere looking for him? What a tragedy, when one woman's joy came as a result of another woman's sorrow.

Chapter 26

Moses Varney sat on the edge of his bed and stared at the television screen, mouth hanging open in disbelief. He shook his head slowly from side to side, as if in a trance. The footage had been played over and over for three days now, but each time he saw the hijacked planes hit the World Trade Center towers he was paralyzed by the surrealism of it. Now, he watched the towers crumble to the ground once again, but still felt a jolt in his heart. *The almighty US of A. Unbelievable!*

Varney took a sip of his cold Club Beer and looked at the news station's images of the hijackers who had been identified so far. Each of those men woke up that morning and knew he was going to give up his life for what he believed in, Varney thought. Did they think about the innocent people they would take down with them? he wondered. How did they justify it? Was it all right in the eyes of God if it was done for a cause they believed was just? What would they say at the final judgment—that one-person Truth Commission in the hereafter? He had asked all these questions of himself during the past decade, and very often in the last few days. Varney thought now of the juvenile delinquents and what Judge Dagoseh was helping them get away with. The judge was simply putting all missing persons and abduction complaints on the back burner—the Simeons and the Alphonsos who had already seen too much as child soldiers and would now be involuntary manpower for the cause. Would their sacrifice really help improve things for future generations? Or would it all be in vain? Varney contemplated his own life. All those years trying to lead his people out of subjugation, and what did he have to show for it? He had to face the truth: Things had definitely gotten worse instead of better. The poor were poorer, and violence was not the way to a more just society. The chief always said the problem was that in Liberia the oppressed don't want to be free; they want to be oppressors too. Maybe he was right.

Varney stood up and stepped across the small room to the dresser. He opened the top drawer and took out a small plastic bag with a bit of white powder in it. *Almost finished!* A bit panicked, he glanced at the room door, which was locked from the outside. The mission had been postponed, the chief had told him, and he was to remain in the Paynesville house until further notice. He snorted the coke and laughed quietly. If this was their idea of punishment he didn't mind at all. Beer, cocaine, digital satellite TV...no problem! He wasn't going to waste another ounce of energy caring anymore. When this was all over, he was going to settle down, make amends with those he hurt, and turn his life around. Maybe he would even take a correspondence course and become an advocate for poor laborers after all.

Varney returned to the bed and flipped between Sky News, CNN, and BBC World while the powder worked its magic. All three stations were covering the same breaking news. Varney marveled at the audacity of the hijackers again. What if one or two of them had changed their minds? he wondered. The whole operation would have been messed up. "There is no place for traitors in a revolution," he said aloud, shaking his head. Truly, traitors were the lowest people on earth. What if he had not caught those twelve guys at Duluma? The nerve of them—plotting to betray him and expose the camp to enemy factions! No one messes with Commander Cobra! They deserved to be beheaded, each and every one of them. The one he picked to use as an example for the cadets reminded him of the uncle he lived with after his parents' death. The uncle was a wimp of a man who feared his Congo boss like a slave feared his master. In fact he was worse than a slave; with a slave there was resentment right alongside the fear, but with his uncle there was nothing to redeem his dignity. Yes sir, yes sir, exploit me sir... His uncle couldn't even stand up to his own wife! For two years that woman made Varney do all the work around the house and yard, including work her children were responsible for before his arrival. She also beat him regularly. After two full years of her refusing to send him to school, and his uncle doing nothing about it, he finally ran away and lived on the streets.

Varney wiped away the tears that suddenly stung his eyes. It wasn't too hard to hustle in those days, but the humiliation of having to steal and of having to eat the leftovers of strangers still hurt. Back then, he knew there was a better way to live and could see that education was his way out. At the time, it was well-known that to cut down on vagrancy and pick-pocketing, *grona* boys were being rounded up and sent to Boys Town in Schiefflin. Boys Town would be a chance for him to go back to school and to get vocational training. He had nothing else, and, fortunately, he had no trouble getting himself caught and sent there.

A noise outside the door to his room snapped Varney out of his thoughts. He listened for some communication or a jingle of keys, but there was nothing.

He could have sworn he heard footsteps. "Who's out there?" he called, hoping his cocaine was about to be replenished.

But there was no answer.

Part Three

Peace is a Reward

Chapter 27

It was a late Sunday afternoon and Bendu, Siatta and Terrance were relaxing together for the first time since Bendu had moved into the Mamba Point apartment. The cook had come back from the market with some huge red snappers, and, with the jazzy tunes of Ella Fitzgerald playing in the background, they had had a serious Sunday brunch. The table was laid out with hot buttery cornbread, eggs and bacon, boiled plantain and cassava, fish in a peppery onion and tomato gravy, freshly-squeezed orange juice, and a seasonal fruit salad. Bendu had said beforehand she wouldn't eat too much because she was going out to dinner with Calvin. But the food was just too irresistible, and now her stomach was so full all she could do was lay on the recliner to daydream and wait for her date. She and Calvin had been spending a lot of time together lately, mostly in the afternoons when they worked together on his second *World Journal* article. The first article on PIP had just been published, complete with great color photographs, and she had sent clips with her follow-up letters to potential donors and partners. This new one was on the peace education center's HIV and AIDS work, and Tenneh was the focus—a young woman who became HIV-positive when she was a victim of war-time sexual assault.

Terrance got up to look through the music CDs for something else to play, and Bendu decided to take a nap. She put the recliner further back and was just about to doze off when she heard Siatta call her name. Her sister was asking about her plans for the night.

"We're going to Beirut Restaurant," she replied.

Siatta gave her a sly look. "I know *that*," she said. "I meant where are you sleeping tonight?"

Bendu picked up a slipper and threw it at her. "Right here in your guest room!" she answered, smiling. "Alone!"

Siatta and Terrance laughed, and for a moment, from where Bendu sat, they looked like a happy couple. Bendu thought about Calvin and tried to picture the two of them growing old together. *Is that what I want? Will I be happy?* But she was distracted from her thoughts by the housekeeper, Sarah, who was heading toward the kitchen with a pile of newspapers in her arms. Curious, Bendu asked the woman what she was doing with the papers.

"Bossman said I should throw them away," Sarah replied.

"They're old," Terrance said, waving Sarah on.

Bendu beckoned to Sarah. "Let me see them."

Terrance reached Bendu in three strides and waved a magazine at her. "Here—read the *BBC Focus on Africa* magazine instead."

Sarah stood still.

"Thanks, I will—but I still want the papers," Bendu insisted. "I want to see what's happening right here in Liberia first." She beckoned for the papers again, and Sarah brought them to her. There were about twenty 8 to 12-page tabloid-sized papers—a week's worth of some of the popular dailies and weeklies: *The Inquirer, The News, The New Liberia, Poll Watch* and *Monrovia Guardian*.

The first paper Bendu looked at had a gruesome picture of a dead and bloated man on the cover, and she tossed it aside in disgust. She picked up another paper and skimmed through the eight pages of stories and ads quickly: Terrorist attacks in the USA...more fighting between rebels and Liberian government forces...LoneStar Cell promising "communication for the nation"...former child soldiers being rehabilitated at the old Boys Town campus...workshop news and pictorials...and sports: football, basketball, and a martial arts tournament.

"Anyone for coffee?" Siatta asked, rising with a stretch and a yawn.

"Good idea, yes," Bendu said.

"I need a cigarette," Terrance said, heading for the balcony.

Bendu picked up all the newspapers and began to sort them by date so she could read them in order. Suddenly, one front page story caught her eye and she screamed.

Siatta came running back from the kitchen with a large knife. "What? What?" she demanded, looking around like a wild woman.

Bendu, speechless, could only gasp and shake the paper with a horrified expression on her face.

Terrance came in from the balcony and ordered his wife to put the knife away. Siatta snatched the paper out of Bendu's hands and scanned the front. Bendu jabbed at the story with a trembling finger. Siatta drew it close and read aloud:

BODY OF VICTIM IDENTIFIED
The body found on Monday in the St. John River has
been positively identified as that of Moses P.N. Varney.
The 54-year-old political activist was identified by a
hotel clerk who saw his photo in *The Inquirer* and
recognized him as a recent guest. According to the
coroner's report, Varney was killed by a bullet to the
head. Investigators do not know whether Varney's
death was murder or a suicide.

"That brother killed himself," Terrance declared.

Bendu put her hands on her head. "Stop, stop! This is
too much. What's the date on that paper?"

Siatta looked at it. "Wednesday, September 19." She looked
over at her husband. "You didn't see this story Terrance?"

"I don't read that junk."

Siatta sucked her teeth. "You buy them for what? The
pictures?"

Bendu wondered the same thing while she rummaged around
for the first paper she had tossed aside. It was dated Tuesday,
September 18. Now she noticed a small passport photo near the
gruesome one of the dead body. "So, they found him on Monday,
published the photos on Tuesday, and he was identified later
the same day by the hotel clerk. Today is Sunday. Why haven't
the police contacted me or Counselor Gray? Or any of us? They
know we've been looking for this man all over the place!"

"Maybe *they* did it," Siatta suggested.

"Killed him?"

"Yeah."

"Don't be silly," Terrance said. "Why would they do such
a thing?"

"I don't know," said Siatta. "But the fact that they never
called…"

"I'm telling you—that brother probably killed himself," Terrance said again.

Bendu frowned. "Commander Cobra? I don't know."

"He was tough, but you never know what's in somebody's heart," Siatta said. "Maybe all the things he did finally overwhelmed his conscience."

Bendu sat down. "This is unbelievable."

"Could there be a connection with the government?" Siatta wondered.

"Maybe his work in Monrovia had something to do with them," Bendu said.

Siatta nodded. "That would certainly explain why they never really pursued him."

"Let's think about this a bit," Bendu said. "Calvin once told me Varney might have been here trafficking arms. People doing that kind of thing always have to watch their backs. What if —"

"Why waste your time speculating?" Terrance interrupted. "The man is dead. Be happy and move on. Isn't that what you wanted?"

Bendu was appalled. "No, of course not! How can you say that?"

"Well you *should* be happy. He's dead now, so you don't have to worry any more. You can even go back home."

Bendu and Siatta both looked at Terrance as if he was out of his mind, and he quickly added, with a laugh, "Oh, I'm *not* saying I don't want you to stay here with us. Stay as long as you like!" But no one laughed with him.

"You are missing the point Terrance," Bendu said curtly. "I just think it's really strange that the police haven't called us. I want to get to the bottom of this."

"There you go again. You women always want to dig deep. Looking for what, I don't know. Well, I'm done with it. I'm going for a drive." He strode out the front door in a huff, lighting a cigarette as he went, and slamming the door shut.

"What was that?" Bendu asked.

Siatta shrugged.

"'Women always want to dig deep?' Did you confront him?"

"No, it must be the guilt talking to him."

Bendu picked up the newspaper and read the story again. *Unbelievable.* "And what if I hadn't looked at the papers today?" she asked aloud.

"God works in mysterious ways."

"Seriously. And you mean to tell me Terrance didn't see these stories?"

"Well apparently no one else we know saw them either. Must be all the news about what happened in America last week. But I told you—he's been up to something lately. He was probably too preoccupied."

The world is surely coming to an end, Bendu thought, as she headed to her room to get ready for the evening. She decided since Calvin was coming over soon, she would just wait and tell him about Cobra in person. The warm bath calmed her shaken nerves somewhat, but her hands were still trembling a bit as she put on a long African print dress with thin straps and a matching jacket. Jewelry was simple: a thin chain with a small mask locket and matching earrings in the classy, dark 18-karat gold from normal days. Bendu inspected herself in the full-length mirror and sprayed some oil sheen on her tiny curls.

"Cute!" Siatta exclaimed, when Bendu returned to the living room.

"Very pretty," Terrance agreed. He had come back from his drive with a smile and some ice cream from Shark's as a peace offering.

"Thanks." Bendu glanced over at the clock on the mantle. Ten to seven.

"You're ready on time," Terrance remarked. "I wish more women were like you," he said, giving Siatta a playfully accusing look.

"Well, Calvin is always right on time," Bendu said. The doorbell rang before she had finished speaking. "See? He's even a bit early tonight." She picked up the Tuesday newspaper to show to Calvin, and headed toward the door. "Don't bother with the intercom; I'll just run down."

Bendu held on to the banister and walked down the stairs quickly. When she reached the lobby she saw two policemen waiting for someone, but there was no sign of Calvin. Puzzled, she turned to talk to the receptionist, but the two police officers accosted her.

"Bendu Lewis?"

"Yes?" She eyed them suspiciously.

The shorter, older man spoke. "We have a warrant for your arrest."

Bendu stepped back and put her hands on her hips. "Is this some kind of joke?" she asked. Just then a loud banging on the door to the lobby made her turn to look. *Calvin! Thank God!* Bendu motioned for the receptionist to let him in. He was at her side in two seconds.

"What's going on here?" Calvin demanded.

"They're arresting me!" Bendu told him.

Calvin glared at the men. "Arresting her for what?" he asked them.

The older man spoke again. "For the murder of Moses Varney."

Chapter 28

Bendu was indignant when the police officer pulled a pair of handcuffs from his belt and reached out to grab her wrist. She stepped back angrily and glared at him. "What on earth do you think you're doing?"

"You didn't hear me? We have a warrant for your arrest!" the officer repeated.

"You've got to be joking." Calvin said. He turned to the receptionist: "Did you call Mr. Clarke?"

"No sir."

"What good are you people? Go up and call the man!"

"I'm not supposed to leave my desk sir."

"Then send a guard. Quickly!"

The girl went outside and called the building security guards. One guard ran up and the other stood nearby.

"Don't try that with us," the policeman with the warrant said to Calvin, grabbing Bendu by the arm.

Bendu pulled her arm out of his grasp. "Don't you dare touch me!"

"Don't try what?" Calvin asked the man.

"We don't care who you know," the officer said. "This is a country of laws, not of men."

"And *you* don't try that rhetorical nonsense with me." Calvin sucked his teeth. "What damn laws are you talking about? Leave the girl alone!" He pulled Bendu toward him and glared at the officer.

Just then, Siatta came bounding down the stairs, followed by Terrance and the building's security guard.

"Good evening gentlemen. What's going on here?" Terrance asked.

The arresting officer cleared his throat and stood at attention. "Yes sir, chief. We have a warrant for this woman's arrest. We need to question her about the Moses Varney case."

"Let me see the warrant." Terrance looked it over and handed it back to the man. "Where are you taking her?"

"Central."

Siatta was appalled. "You mean you're going to *let* them take her?"

Terrance shrugged. "What can I do baby? The warrant is legitimate."

"Can't you call the Chief of Police? Isn't he your friend?" Siatta was almost in tears.

"What did I tell you Siatta? I can't do that. Besides, I haven't been in touch with Kesselly for ages."

"Bendu is your family and she's going to jail! What was all that big mouth at the hospital? Suddenly you're Mr. Play-By-The-Rules?"

Terrance lowered his eyes and shrugged helplessly.

Calvin took charge. "Listen—it's okay. Siatta, we'll both go along. There's no basis for this arrest. We'll straighten it out at the station."

"I'll wait here in case there's anything," Terrance said.

"You do that," Siatta said with a scowl.

Bendu refused to ride in the police car, and the officers had no choice but to lead the way to the Police Headquarters as she and the others followed in Calvin's SUV.

"Well, at least they brought a car to get me," she said, trying to make light of the situation.

Calvin grinned. "As opposed to the pick-up truck with twenty officers crammed in the back?" he asked.

"That would have been bad too," Bendu said, laughing. "But the worst is when they come to harass you and then want *you* to pay for their transportation back or for a taxi to wherever they want to take you."

Siatta shook her head. "Only in Liberia."

Bendu opened her purse and reached in for her cell phone. "I'd better call Counselor Gray and have him meet us there. Thank God for LoneStar—I don't know *how* we managed without phones for so long!"

At the National Police Headquarters, the police officer and his partner led them past the non-functioning metal detector and up two flights of worn-down concrete stairs. Bendu had been such a frequent visitor during her pursuit of Varney that a couple of people recognized her and greeted her as she walked by. The officers led them to a long bench in the hallway outside the director's wing.

Much to Bendu's surprise and relief, Counselor Reeves came to her rescue himself, with Counselor Gray tagging along looking a bit unsure of himself. Reeves got a quick update from Calvin, and then began to berate the two arresting officers, insisting that they had no evidence whatsoever to arrest Bendu as a suspected murderer, and reminding them that they were not even sure the man had been murdered. His quarrelling brought the director of police, Edwin Kesselly, out of his office. Chief Kesselly had a frown on his face, but then relaxed and smiled when he saw the lawyer.

"Reeves! Is that you causing a disturbance in my office?"

Counselor Reeves laughed and the two men gave each other a hearty Liberian handshake: a slap of the palms followed by an intricate duet of their middle fingers and thumbs to end in a loud 'snap!' Kesselly greeted Calvin, Siatta and Bendu as well.

Well, this is getting better, Bendu thought.

Counselor Reeves cleared his throat and spoke with concern. "Chief, my client here has been wrongly arrested."

"Reeves, Reeves!" Kesselly gave a jolly Santa-like laugh. "Let me make it clear: Miss Lewis is not being arrested. We only invited her here so she can clarify some things for us. Lieutenant Tarpeh will be arriving soon to ask her some questions."

Calvin stepped forward. "And she may leave afterward?"

"Of course!" Kesselly said, looking over at Bendu with a smile. "This is no place for such a pretty little thing to spend the night." He turned back to Reeves. "In fact, this is no place for *me* to spend the night. I'm on my way home in a few minutes."

Siatta spoke up. "May I have your card Chief Kesselly, in case we need to call you?"

"Of course," he said, opening his wallet. "Anything for you, Mrs. Clarke."

Siatta looked at the business card he handed her. "That number's easy to remember," she remarked.

"Almost as easy as 911," he said, with a wink. "Call anytime. And greetings to your husband."

The police director left soon afterward, like he said he would, but by the time Lieutenant Tarpeh arrived, Bendu had indeed spent the night at the police station. They had been moved to a sort of holding room, where several suspected criminals and a couple of drunkards were brought in one by one as the night progressed. Reeves had gone home at midnight, asking to be called when he was needed, but Calvin and Siatta had stayed by Bendu's side. It was almost dawn when Lieutenant Tarpeh showed up, and they were all hungry, tired, and livid. They were even angrier when Tarpeh insisted on questioning Bendu alone. They argued bitterly, but in the end she relented just so they could get the whole thing over with and get back home.

Bendu followed Lieutenant Tarpeh into his downstairs office and stood by while he rummaged about in his file cabinet. She heard footsteps and turned to see a security guard dressed in black and armed with an M-16 enter the office. He stood guard by the door and Bendu turned her back to him. *What do they think I am? Some kind of criminal with an escape risk?* Tarpeh pulled out a file and turned to look at her.

"We meet again," he said, sounding both surprised and pleased—as if they were acquaintances and this was their first time seeing each other in a while.

"Why didn't you let me know when Varney was found?" Bendu inquired.

"*I'm* asking the questions today, Miss Lewis. Please...sit down."

Bendu sat down and folded her arms.

Lieutenant Tarpeh opened the file, took out a form, and pulled a pen out of his shirt pocket. He twirled it around slowly while he looked at her. "Do you own a weapon, Miss Lewis?"

"No."

"When did you last see Moses Varney?"

"About three weeks ago. How long has he been dead?"

"I was hoping *you* could tell me that."

Bendu took a deep breath and kept her eyes on the officer. *Sometimes the best response is no response.* She had read that somewhere.

"You say you last saw Varney three weeks ago."

"Right. The night he attacked me."

"I bet that made you angry."

"Of course."

"Angry enough to kill him?"

"Look, I did not kill the man, okay? Don't be ridiculous."

Tarpeh frowned. "Are you insulting me?"

"Don't you have the coroner's report? Don't they estimate the time of death?"

Tarpeh stared at her for a while, then picked up a file and glanced through it. "Where were you last weekend at about three in the afternoon?"

"Saturday I was at the Palm Hotel's rooftop restaurant, and on Sunday I was at home."

"Do you have proof?"

"I was with a friend Saturday. With friends and family Sunday."

Tarpeh cleared his throat and chewed on his pen. "People who would be willing to cover for you."

Bendu rolled her eyes.

"Do you have receipts?" he asked her.

"Look, why don't you go and ask the people who work at those places?"

"Don't worry, we will do that."

"Good."

"And you will stay in detention until the results of our investigation are in." He put the cap back on his pen and placed it in his shirt pocket.

Bendu blinked back tears and refused to meet his eye.

"Who's laughing now, Miss Lewis?" Tarpeh asked quietly, as he put the file away.

Chapter 29

Bendu stomped along as Lieutenant Tarpeh led her upstairs with the armed guard following close behind.

"What's going on here?" she asked Tarpeh. "Men like Varney are allowed to go about with impunity, and *I* am being punished for something I didn't even do?"

He didn't answer, and she wondered how long their stupid investigation would take. She didn't have time to sit in their police station wasting her time. Bendu shook her head. *ADT*, she thought. *This is a perfect example.* In spite of her frustration she smiled now at the thought of the little joke they always told Liberians in the diaspora who inquired about the security situation in the country. 'Oh, we have the ADT security system in place here,' they would answer. 'Oh really?' the unsuspecting person would ask, pleasantly surprised to hear the familiar brand name. 'Yeah—ADT,' they would answer. 'Any Damn Thing can happen!' Bendu chuckled and Tarpeh looked at her sharply.

By now they had reached the lobby of the building, where a number of employees were arriving to begin the workday.

Calvin and Siatta were waiting on a bench, apparently expecting her. They rose and rushed forward to meet her.

Lieutenant Tarpeh stood looking at them embrace each other. When they all turned to look at him he said "You know what? I'm going to let Miss Lewis go on her own recognizance."

Bendu gave him a scornful look, but didn't say anything.

"I hope this is the end of it," Calvin said to him.

"Well, we'll be in touch," Tarpeh promised, as the three turned to leave.

Bendu didn't break down until they were out of the building. Calvin held her in his arms and comforted her as she cried. She was more annoyed than anything else, and quickly regained her composure.

No one spoke much on the way to Mamba Point, and Bendu was able to think a bit. The closer they got to their destination, the more she realized what she needed to do.

"I'm moving back to my own place," she said quietly, as much to herself as to Siatta and Calvin.

"No Bendu," Siatta protested. "Why? Can't you wait until all of this is finished?"

Calvin agreed. "It's not a good idea for you to be alone yet," he said.

Bendu shook her head firmly. "I've made up my mind," she said. "Terrance was right: Cobra is dead and I have nothing to fear anymore."

Siatta tried again to talk her out of moving, but Calvin stopped her, and they stayed quiet until they were heading up the hill toward the apartment.

"I guess we'll need to reschedule our date," Calvin said to Bendu as they approached the apartment building.

"Sure. I'm sorry about all this Calvin. I'll call you, okay?"

He smiled and leaned toward her for a kiss, then waited until she and Siatta had entered the building before he drove off.

A phone was ringing as Bendu and Siatta opened the apartment door. It was Terrance's phone on the dining room table.

Siatta yelled for him down the hallway, but there was no answer.

"He must have gone out and forgotten it," Bendu said.

When the phone stopped ringing, Siatta picked it up and started pressing buttons.

"What are you doing?" Bendu asked.

"Last ten calls."

"Siatta!"

"No. I want to see who he's been calling, and who's been calling him." She pressed a few more buttons, raised her eyebrows, and frowned.

"What is it?" Bendu asked.

Siatta shook her head and put the phone down, but didn't respond. She looked troubled, but Bendu decided not to pry.

"Are you still determined to go back home?" Siatta asked.

"It's the best thing," Bendu replied. "Besides, you and Terrance need to have a serious talk, and I don't want to be in your way."

Chapter 30

After the contrite security guards assured Bendu—much to her amusement— that they were now "on special alert" for rogues and other intruders, she walked into her house alone. It wasn't until she was inside and saw the vase full of dead flowers that she realized the palaver hut with its romantic arch had been removed from the courtyard while she was away. She dragged her suitcase to her room and resisted the urge to flop down on the bed and go to sleep. She went back out and double-checked all the windows and doors to make sure they were locked, and to make sure no one was in there with her. At the door of the second bedroom she paused and tried to imagine how she would fix it up for Baby Girl. What would she like at ten? Ruffles? Flowers? Teddy bears? Something more grown-up? Was she too big for doll babies? What was her favorite color? What kind of music did she like? Was she even alive?

Bendu turned away from the room. What if Baby Girl was alive but wouldn't forgive her? What if the murder accusations by the police became public and made ICRC stop the tracing or decide reunification would not be in the best interests of the child?

She put the nagging questions at the back of her mind and got out her cell phone. She had to call Agnes to say she wasn't coming in.

Agnes answered on the first ring. "Bendu! I was just about to call you. Did you see the article on Tenneh?"

"It's out?"

"It's out in style! Good things come to those who wait, but *great* things come to those who act. You should see your messages here at the office! Every single newspaper has called, the people from Health & Social Welfare want to see us, and Jonathan Paye-Layleh wants to do a story for the BBC!"

Bendu was speechless.

"That's not the best of it," Agnes went on.

"No?"

"No. A couple of donor organizations have called too!"

Bendu laughed. "Donors calling *us*?"

Agnes was ecstatic. "Yes! Bendu, you and Calvin did well o. This is going to be our saving grace."

"Well, it will certainly help us help ourselves," Bendu said. "That was the idea. How's Tenneh taking the attention?"

"She's okay for now. Her counselor is with her and she has a few people standing by her side, but..."

"But what?"

"Some of her neighbors worry that they might get HIV just from being around her. They don't understand that it can only be transmitted through contaminated sexual fluids or infected blood."

"We should do some community awareness there as soon as possible. How is Tenneh doing?"

"She's doing fine. Still as cheerful as ever," Agnes replied.

The two talked for a little while longer, and Bendu hung up with mixed feelings. Her happiness about the success of the article was tempered by the shock of Varney's murder, and regrets about not forgiving him outright when he was still alive. She also felt sorry for Siatta and her marital problems, and a deep worry for the child she had abandoned at Duluma and might never know. All that, plus the humiliation of being arrested and harassed. It was too much. She flung herself onto the bed and cried until no more tears would come.

When Bendu finally found the strength to get out of bed, she did it with a renewed sense of purpose and specific plans.

First, she went to the kitchen, put some water from the barrel into a big pot on the stove, and lit the gas burner under it. Then she went out to the small living room and looked around. Everything seemed to be in order, but the rattan furniture and the bookcases needed a little dusting. Her collection of Madonna and Child statuettes made of wood, bronze, stone, and other materials was still there. When she told people she didn't know why she was so drawn to them, she wasn't lying. But now she knew the reason. All these years the statuettes had challenged her. They had made her remember what she was trying to forget. And now, as always, they gave her comfort and hope. No matter where Baby Girl was, whether she was dead or alive, rich or poor, she was in the arms of God. Bendu saw that all her pictures were still there too, on the walls and bookcases and little tables. There was the whole Lewis family together, Granny May dressed in white for a Mother's Day celebration at church, a precious black and white picture of herself at age five with Siatta and Benji, and several photos of her with Jonah.

Bendu sat on the couch, closed her eyes and thought of Calvin and about the way he looked at her. About the things he saw in her face and in her demeanor. Last night at the police station, they had some time alone when Siatta went out to get them something to eat. He had told her that he loved her and would be there to help her get over any obstacle on her way to recovery. He said he would fight every impatient cell in his body to wait for her, if she could assure him that he had a chance. He was sincere—of that she had no doubt. But there was still a wall she couldn't get over, and now it had nothing to do with her war-time past. No. Now it had everything to do with her future, and with the future of Liberia. Calvin was wonderful but he was weighed down by his own past and his own prejudices, and he couldn't even see it. To him, the continuing suffering of the masses could be justified, and Bendu didn't know if he would ever be able to open his heart to an individual from the other side of his clear line between classes. Even with sweet Tenneh... He had exercised great talent to get the girl to reveal her heart, but he failed to see her as the innocent victim that she was—not just of the war, but of birth and of circumstance. He moved the world with Tenneh's story, but his own outlook didn't budge. Despite all this though, Bendu found it reassuring that their courtship had almost reached a place inside her that she had believed was reserved for only one person. Jonah was gone, but she *was* still capable of loving and of being loved.

Bendu took a deep breath, opened her eyes, walked over to the bookcase and picked up her engagement photo. It was a copy of the one she kept on her desk at the office. There

Jonah was, smiling at the camera, and there she was, gazing at his ear with love in her eyes. It looked as if she was telling him a secret—something that pleased him. Bendu blinked and held the picture closer. He was happy because *she* was so happy. That's what he had been telling her before the photographer came by. I want to keep that smile on your face, he had said, forever and for always; you just tell me what I need to do. Now, she drew the picture up to her lips and kissed him. "Thank you, Jonah," she whispered. She went around the room and gathered the other photos of them together, but left his graduation portrait of which he was so proud. This one, she decided, would help her remember his accomplishments and remind her to create the future that they envisioned for Liberia. She hugged the frames to her chest and went into her room, where there were two more pictures to add to the ones in her arms. She put all of them in a sturdy shoebox, and placed the box out of sight on the shelf of her wardrobe.

Her next stop was the bathroom. A roach had crawled into the tub while she was away—probably looking for water to drink—and had died there. Bendu swept it up with a small broom and dustpan, then washed the tub and placed a bucket in it, half filled with cold water from the barrel. She took the dustpan to the kitchen, and returned with the hot water from the stove. She poured the hot water into the bucket and tested it to make sure it was okay for her bath. Then she opened the cabinet under the sink and took out the mirror that she had placed there when Moses Varney sauntered into town bringing her nightmares and her self-loathing back. She put the mirror back on the wall above the sink where it belonged, and, standing straight and tall, looked herself in the eyes and smiled.

Chapter 31

A couple of weeks went by, and Lieutenant Tarpeh's promise to continue investigating Bendu for murder proved to be an empty threat. Even with that, and with Moses Varney gone, Bendu was still a little nervous whenever the doorbell rang, and she never entered the house or went to bed without first checking every door and window. These days the last thought on her mind before she went to sleep was always the same: *Baby Girl*. The tracing assistant at ICRC said sometimes it took just days to trace someone, and sometimes much longer. And of course, Bendu knew, some people never connected at all. You just had to have the right mixture of determination and luck. There was no news yet, but Bendu tried not to despair. She hoped someone, somewhere, would know at least one of the women for whom she was searching—one of the women who could tell her where Baby Girl was.

To try to keep her mind off her worries, Bendu immersed herself in the day-to-day activities at Peace in Practice. The center now served close to 50 clients, and the Truth Project that Agnes had conceived was proving to be a major success. In addition to the sharing of experiences, Agnes had come up with the idea of recruiting volunteers to serve as surrogate perpetrators and victims. The surrogates were used for victims who needed to forgive someone face to face, and for perpetrators who needed to beg forgiveness from those hurt or killed. The volunteers were great actors, and it was a powerful and empowering exercise for everyone involved.

Bendu's family and friends all seemed to be busy too, and she hadn't seen her sister or Terrance since the day she moved out of their Mamba Point apartment.

One Saturday morning, just as she was thinking of going over to Siatta's place, Siatta showed up on her doorstep looking distraught.

Bendu's jaw dropped open when she heard that Terrance was the one who had prompted Chief Kesselly to have her arrested.

"Are you absolutely sure about this?" Bendu asked her sister. "My own brother-in-law?"

"I've been playing detective for the past two weeks. I know." Siatta paced up and down the small living room.

"Siatta. Sit, please."

"I can't sit down. I'm too upset."

Bendu paced along with her. "Why would my own brother-in-law do this to me?"

Siatta shook her head. "I have no idea. It was that day when he stormed out of the apartment and came back with ice cream for us."

"Did he know Moses Varney?"

Siatta shrugged. "I don't know. I don't know anything anymore."

Bendu led the way to her bedroom, and, at her prompting, Siatta sat down on the bed beside her and told the whole story.

The day they returned home from Police Headquarters after her arrest and release, Bendu learned, Siatta had seen Kesselly's number among both the 'Received Calls' and 'Dialled Numbers' lists in Terrance's phone.

"He told us he hadn't spoken to the police chief for ages!" Bendu exclaimed.

"And that's not all," Siatta continued. "Since then I've eavesdropped on him and heard some pretty strong evidence of his involvement. I also uncovered other troubling things."

"Girlfriends?"

"At least two of them, but that's not the important thing right now. I think Terrance had something to do with helping Cobra avoid the writ of arrest, but he swears he knows nothing about the murder."

Bendu raised her eyebrows. "You confronted him?"

"I was too mad. If he didn't know Varney, he certainly knew some of Varney's friends."

The two paused for a bit and Bendu tried to take in all this new information. "What are we going to do?" she finally asked her sister.

Siatta grabbed a pillow and hugged it close. "I don't know Bendu. I really don't know."

"Do you still love him?"

"That's not the point."

"It's not?"

"We've been together for too long. Plus…Mommie and Daddy love him."

Without warning, Bendu felt something catch in her throat and sudden tears stung her eyes.

Siatta reached over and held her gently. "I'm sorry Bendu," she said softly. "If I could change what Terrance did —"

Bendu shook her head vigorously. "It's not about Terrance."

"What is it then?"

"Mommie and Daddy," Bendu said.

"What about Mommie and Daddy?"

"They think it was my fault that Granny May died like that," Bendu answered, the tears flowing freely now.

"No!" Siatta cried out, astonished.

"Yes!" Bendu insisted.

Siatta grabbed her by the shoulders and shook her. "No! No! No! Bendu, I have to apologize for what happened —"

"I told you—what Terrance did is not your fault."

"Not that. It's about the year you were missing," Siatta explained. "No one in the family has ever once asked you about it."

Bendu started to say something, but Siatta cut her off. "No, don't say it's okay. It's not okay. We should have told you that we would be willing to listen whenever you were ready to talk." Her voice was soft as she continued. "All of us feel bad about it Bendu. We're so wrong. You know, it's hard listening to the stories of strangers, but it's even harder to imagine or know that someone you love went through it too."

Bendu breathed evenly and got up and walked across the room, trying to take in what she was hearing.

"That's why Mommie and Daddy look at you or avoid you the way they do sometimes," Siatta said. "It's *not* because of Granny May at all."

Bendu turned and looked at her sister. "And Cousin Rebecca?"

"Same thing." Siatta shook her head sadly. "We couldn't even imagine...and deep down I think we didn't even want to know. It's been really hard for them—for all of us—not knowing what to do or say to help you."

Bendu nodded. Her lips were trembling, but she managed a shaky smile before the dam within her broke. *All these years, and finally...validation from my family!* Her legs suddenly felt too weak to support her, but before they buckled, Siatta was there. They embraced tightly, each weeping for herself as well as for the other.

"One more thing..." Siatta said after pulling away and wiping her sister's face gently. "You need to forgive yourself for Orlando. Cousin Rebecca forgave you a long time ago, but we know you're still blaming yourself for what happened to him."

"But if I hadn't wanted to leave so badly —"

"If nothing," Siatta interrupted. "Good decisions, bad decisions...sometimes it just doesn't matter. Sometimes you just have to do what you have to do. Two people made decisions that day you left Sumoville—you *and* Orlando. Even Granny May."

Bendu wiped her eyes. "Cousin Rebecca forgave me?"

"Completely." Siatta smiled. "Goodness! How many times does she have to tell you not to worry about it?"

Bendu didn't look convinced. "How *could* she forgive me?"

"She's Cousin Rebecca and she loves you," Siatta said matter-of-factly. "How could she *not* forgive you? I doubt she ever really blamed you to begin with."

Bendu thought about it and managed to smile a little.

"That's better," Siatta encouraged. "Hey!" she remarked suddenly, peering at Bendu's head. "There's hardly a scar where your stitches were! I almost forgot you were hurt!"

Bendu smiled a little more. Yes. The scar on her head was barely visible, and now the wounds of her heart were finally going to start healing as well.

Chapter 32

As the Christmas season drew closer, the Harmattan wind from the north began to cool the mornings and evenings, like a set of parentheses around the hot days. The fighting between rebels and government forces grew more intense, and President Taylor grew more intolerant of any opposition—or 'detractors' as all critics were called. There was a constant migration to the rapidly growing IDP camps on the outskirts of Monrovia, and things got even busier at Peace in Practice. With Calvin's widely-read articles had come recognition and several visits from other humanitarian organizations—and because of their innovative Truth Project, PIP soon won more grants to support and extend their work.

Sometimes, despite all the action around her, Bendu was a bit aloof and Agnes would ask her whether she was thinking of Duluma or worrying about Baby Girl. It had been a while since she had filled in the tracing request at ICRC, and the wait was agonizing. Twice Agnes urged her to do the letter-writing assignment as a way of moving forward with her healing process, and twice Bendu promised that she would. But work was just too demanding and she kept putting it off.

Once in a while Bendu's thoughts did drift to Duluma— that place of darkness and gloom that so many had endured. Calvin had once told her that Monrovia in April 1980 was *his* Duluma. She knew exactly what he meant.

Calvin was in Freetown now, covering the progress of the Sierra Leone war crimes tribunal for *World Journal*. Bendu thought it was just as well. He was not too happy with her decision to "just be friends", but was not prepared to change his views and had left in a sullen mood. She hoped the physical separation would give him some time to get over it.

Despite the domestic troubles in Liberia, the sights and sounds of the season proceeded as usual. The exchange rate gradually went down as low as 42 to 1, and the streets began to fill with small merchants and people of all types hawking all manner of goods: cheap plastic toys, stuffed animals, baby shoes that squeaked with every step, cell phone accessories, dishes, lappas, wooden nativity sets and other carvings, and 2-piece outfits for kids made from colorful scraps from the local tailor shops. Some sellers made a space for themselves on the sidewalks, and others walked through neighborhoods shouting to let people know what they had. Rumors that something big was going to happen to coincide with the anniversary of the beginning of the civil war proved false, and Christmas came and went with no major crisis.

Several weeks into the New Year, however, the fighting erupted in several close towns almost simultaneously. One incident was near Gardnersville, and the proximity of the rockets and machine-gun fire caused a panic that rippled in waves toward the center of town. Throughout Monrovia people ran helter-skelter. Not everyone had heard the shooting so most people didn't know what was happening and no one knew which way to go for safety. It was chaos.

Siatta was on her way home when the confusion broke out and was alarmed to see schoolchildren running scared amidst the adults, and a stream of people walking quickly toward the American Embassy with bundles, pots, and even mattresses on their heads. She tried to call Bendu and Terrance right away, but apparently everyone with a cell phone had the same idea; with only one network in the country—and less than a year old at that—the phone lines were jammed. Siatta would later tell Bendu she had never been so scared in her life. She had run into the apartment, she said, grabbed nothing but her passport, and literally run around in circles praying madly until Terrance finally showed up.

Shortly after the Gardnersville incident, a State of Emergency was declared despite much public objection. People feared that the government would use it as an excuse to crack down on dissidents and human rights activists. It was in the middle of all this commotion that Eva Lewis returned home to prepare for her once annual April pilgrimage to Benji's grave. Because of the civil war she had not made the special visit in ten years.

Although it had been twenty-two years since Benji was killed, April was still always a tough month for the Lewis family. Everyone dealt with the tragedy of the coup, the subsequent killing of Benji, and the infamous April 22 executions on the beach in their own way, and mostly in silence. But Eva Lewis was known to sink into a dark and tearful depression for weeks. As soon as she arrived, though, she announced that things would be different this time. "Yes, I'm here for Benji," she said to her daughters, "but also for you." Then, deliberately avoiding eye contact with anyone, she added "And I'm also here to make preparations for my granddaughter."

Bendu and Siatta didn't know what to make of these surprising declarations. They stood in Siatta's blue guest room now, each holding a heavy designer suitcase, and glanced at each other with looks that expressed doubt. Bendu set her mother's suitcase down and sat on the bed. "Oh Mommie!" she said, with an exaggerated sigh.

"What?" Eva asked, a bit defensively.

Siatta jumped in. "We haven't found the little girl yet, Mommie. Don't add more stress to your life."

Their mother smiled. "Don't worry about me. You two are the ones stressing out. Siatta, you with Terrance, and Bendu...you have *so* much going on. I really mean it when I say I'm here for you this time. Benji's gone, but the two of you are right here, standing in front of me."

Bendu and Siatta glanced at each other again. For twenty-two years now they had felt overshadowed by their dead brother but had grown used to it, in a way.

"How come you can see us now?" Bendu asked quietly.

"I always saw you," Eva replied. "I never stopped seeing you."

"Then what happened Mommie?" Siatta asked. "Why do you always make us feel that your life would be so much better if Benji were still alive?"

Eva looked surprised. "Because it *would* be. Benji was a part of me, and he was...taken away."

Siatta pouted. "And we were not enough?"

"To do what? Fill the void?" Eva shrugged and shook her head. "No, baby. And believe me, I would feel the same way if it had been either one of you."

Bendu put her arms around her mother and Siatta came near to hug her too. They sat like that, the three Lewis women, each lost in her own thoughts and gathering comfort in their embrace.

"Benji loved you both," Eva whispered softly. "Even at twelve, he really loved you."

Bendu smiled. "That's funny—Calvin said the very same thing!"

Eva nodded. "He was there."

Bendu suddenly sat up straight. "What are you talking about Mommie?"

Eva sighed and propped herself comfortably against the pillows.

"Tell us Mommie," Siatta prompted.

Eva spoke quietly. "Well, we knew the soldiers would come for your father after the coup, so we sent the three of you to Calvin's house. His parents were so well-known and so adored by everyone because of the university scholarships they provided every year for underprivileged students. We thought no one would touch them."

"And what happened?" Bendu prompted.

"You don't remember? Some soldiers went there anyway—led by some university students."

The tender mercies of a heathen are cruelty. The old warning that meant it didn't pay to be too kind to certain people flashed into Bendu's mind immediately.

Eva, apparently, had had the same thought. She shrugged. "Maybe they were disgruntled students who didn't get scholarships. I don't know. Anyway, the soldiers made CJ and Angela Daniels *pump tire*—squat and stand, squat and stand, over and over again, and made them chant 'Doe up! Tolbert down! Doe up! Tolbert down!' while they were doing it. Then they made them kneel down on piles of broken glass while their men went in to search the house."

"Search the house for what?"

"They said they were looking for money."

Siatta was puzzled. "And where were *we*?"

"You don't remember?"

"We were too young Mommie!" Bendu almost shouted.

"And you guys never wanted to talk about it." Siatta added. "You told us to let bygones be bygones."

And we did! Bendu realized, with a sinking feeling in her stomach.

Eva looked surprised. "So this is really the first time you're hearing this?"

Bendu was really exasperated this time. "Yes Mommie!" she almost yelled.

Her mother smiled sadly, and Bendu could see the beginning of fine wrinkles in her face. She leaned over and kissed her on the cheek. "It's okay Mommie," she said softly. "Please tell us what happened."

Quietly, Eva finally began to tell her daughters the story of how their brother had given his own life to save theirs.

Benji and Calvin, Eva said, had been looking out of a second-floor bedroom window when the students arrived with the soldiers. When the soldiers dragged CJ and Angela Daniels outdoors and began to strip them, Benji ran to hide his sisters in an overhead storage space while Calvin remained at the window, paralyzed by what was happening to his parents. It wasn't until the men entered the house that Calvin was able to move. He went into one closet, and Benji, having just finished coaxing the girls to be brave and quiet up there no matter what, went into another.

"There was really no better place to hide," Eva said, "and they knew it was only a matter of time before they would be discovered."

"So what happened?" Siatta asked.

"They found Benji first. The one who opened the closet yelled 'Here's their son! Here's their son!' Then someone else said 'Let's carry him down. When we finish with him his ma and pa will tell us where the money is.'"

Eva paused, and Bendu reached out to hold her hand.

Eva spoke in a whisper now. "Calvin said he saw Benji look back once—as if he expected him to come out and claim his rightful title."

"But he didn't get out," Bendu said softly.

"No."

Siatta was incredulous. "He let them take our brother away in his place?"

Eva nodded. "But you know what? What if Calvin *had* come out? The men might have wondered who else was hiding in that room."

"And they might have found *us*," Bendu said.

Eva nodded again. "We believe that's exactly what Benji was thinking when he went along with those men, but that never could console Calvin."

"And so what happened next?" Siatta asked. "How did Benji get shot?"

"That, no one knows for sure. It happened on the staircase as they were going down. Was it deliberate? Was it an accident? Was Benji trying to fight them? Or to escape?" Eva shrugged. "All we know is that it should not have been him going down that staircase."

Calvin's Duluma. Now Bendu really understood.

Chapter 33

⁓

The heavy rains began in the first week of April, cleansing Monrovia and bringing some relief from the tropical heat. It was a time of growth and renewal, and nothing announced it as clearly as the hundreds of "plum" trees everywhere laden with green and ripening mangoes. Bendu didn't believe it would happen, but her mother was like a different woman, and did what she said she would. Eva Lewis spent quality time with her daughters, being cheerful and brightening up their days. There were only two times when she seemed a little morose—the day she hired someone to clean the family plot and whitewash all the graves, and the day she ordered the floral wreaths from Valrica's on UN Drive.

On the 15th of April, the anniversary of Benji's death, they all went to Palm Grove Cemetery together—Bendu and Siatta with their mother. There was already one large wreath propped up on the headstone, and the women knew Calvin had already been there. They stood together at the foot of the grave, and this time it was Bendu and Siatta who broke down while their mother stood like a pillar of strength between them, holding them up with strong arms and an even stronger spirit.

Soon after the pilgrimage to Benji's grave, Bendu's house became a whirlwind of activity. The second bedroom was painted a light pink, and Grandma Eva—as she had started referring to herself—added a border of white flowers along the walls, and made white curtains for the window. It was as if one obsession had replaced the other: the pain of Benji had died, and the promise of Baby Girl was born. Eva had local carpenters from LIPCO make a new bed, a bookcase, a study desk and chair, and a dresser with a mirror—all with the finest wood and craftsmanship. She had brought solid-colored sheet sets from the States with her, and the quilting class at PIP made a pretty quilt and matching pillow shams in white, with pink and yellow flowers and a sky blue border. Bendu was starting to get a little worried that her mother was setting herself up for a big letdown, but Agnes reminded her that faith as small as a mustard seed could move mountains.

Sure enough, as if Eva's faith was the kind needed to set things in motion, Gabriel appeared at Bendu's house the day after Baby Girl's room was finished. The ICRC animators in Ghana had identified a possible match at the Buduburam Refugee Camp, he told them.

Bendu and Eva ushered him in quickly and sat on the edge of the couch in anticipation.

"There wasn't much to go on," Gabriel said, "since you didn't know the child's name."

Bendu could only nod anxiously and squeeze her mother's hand.

It turned out the tracing department had made a connection based on names that they found in the girl's documentation. Gabriel said the girl they found through cross-referencing had been separated from her aunt and grandmother in 1996 when she was around three years old, sometime during the infamous April 6 fighting and the ensuing chaos. Apparently, the family intended to flee Monrovia together on a ship. The little girl made it onto the *Bulk Challenge*, a Nigerian vessel, but her guardian could not be located. All she had with her was a large teddy bear to which she clung as if her life depended on it. The people who took care of her during the ten days at sea, while the ship was refused permission to dock anywhere in West Africa, said she kept asking for her Aunty Oretha and her Grandma Musu.

Bendu held her breath and blinked rapidly.

"It's got to be her!" Eva said.

"Speculation is that the girl's people either got killed somewhere near the port, or got on one of the two other ships that left around the same time as *Bulk Challenge*," Gabriel told them. "But all efforts to trace them in Sierra Leone and Nigeria at that time failed."

"It's got to be her," Eva said again.

"Oretha and Musu. Those are common Liberian names," Bendu said quietly.

Eva looked at her. "At least they're in the right places here. Oretha is the aunt, and Musu is the grandmother."

"The age is off," Bendu said. "She would have been four."

"Maybe she was just small for her age," Gabriel said. "Malnourishment was common among children during the war."

"Maybe she's Hannah's daughter," Bendu whispered to her mother.

"Hannah had a daughter? You didn't tell me that."

"Well, not when I was there. But anything could have happened."

"And what would they have done with *your* daughter?"

"I don't know. Maybe she died."

Eva put her arms around Bendu. "Look, I know you're only trying to protect yourself from disappointment, but don't be ridiculous." She smiled at her daughter, then turned to the tracing assistant and asked, "What's the girl's name?"

Gabriel looked at the information in front of him. "Her first name is May," he said. "Last name, Davies."

Bendu gasped and clutched Gabriel's arm. "May! May was my grandmother's name! I was taken to Duluma the night after she died."

Gabriel smiled. "That's good. That's very good. One more plus for positive verification."

Bendu sat back and looked at her mother, who was smiling through tears of joy. "Mommie, they named her after Granny May!"

"I know, baby, I heard him, I heard him!"

Bendu felt like someone had punched her in the stomach, slapped her in the face, and told her she had won a million dollars all at once. She looked at Gabriel and even he had tears in his eyes.

"The name Davies gave us hope," he said, "because of your Red Cross Message to Hannah Davies."

Bendu nodded and told her mother Davies was the last name of Hannah's rebel "husband". That meant Hannah and Joseph must have stayed together, and were probably the ones who kept Baby Girl.

"So why was she asking only for her Aunty Oretha and Grandma Musu?" Eva wondered.

"I don't know," Bendu said. "Where were Hannah and Joseph by April 6 and how long had Oretha and Ma Musu been in Monrovia with my child?"

"The answers will come slowly," Gabriel said, "and some you'll never get at all. It's amazing that the child knew her last name. Most kids that young don't."

"She's a Lewis girl. She's smart!" Eva said proudly.

Gabriel laughed, and Bendu shook her head and smiled. "Oh this is just unbelievable."

"When can we get her?" Eva asked. "When can my grand-baby come home?"

"Well, hold on. You don't just 'get her' like that," Gabriel answered.

"Okay, what's the procedure?"

"Bendu has to fill out a request for reunification and we have to make sure May is willing to come under her mother's care."

"See if she's willing?"

"Absolutely. The CRC—the United Nations Convention on the Rights of the Child—gives her the right to help make decisions about her own life."

"At ten?" Eva asked, a bit surprised.

"Even younger. Remember now, she's been at the camp about five, six years. She has a family, school, friends—a life."

"But what about her best interests?"

"Well, naturally we want to reunite all children with their families," Gabriel explained to Eva, "but sometimes it's actually in the child's best interest to leave her where she is. Look at what's happening around us now with all this fighting. I'll tell you, even if reunification is approved, we probably will have to wait until the country is more stable."

Eva nodded and sighed.

"Who is she with now?" Bendu asked anxiously.

"A children's home," Gabriel replied.

"What about the people from the ship?"

"They kept May for a while, but they had a large family of their own and had to give her up."

Eva took out a handkerchief and wiped her eyes.

"And if reunification is approved, what will be the next step?" Bendu asked.

"We'll need to meet to discuss the plans and clarify anything that still needs to be clarified," Gabriel told her. "We'll also need to fill out the application forms for the travel documents necessary to get the child out of Ghana and into Liberia as soon as it's safe enough."

"And what do we do in the meantime?" Bendu asked.

"In the meantime, you and May could begin corresponding with each other and exchanging photos," Gabriel answered. "And just be patient," he added with a kind smile. "Whatever is supposed to happen will happen in God's time."

Chapter 34

Bendu got out of the car and sprinted across the sidewalk so she wouldn't get soaked by the heavy September morning rain. Under the awning of the office building, she said good morning to the others taking refuge there, and folded up her umbrella. She stood and watched schoolchildren from B. W. Harris Episcopal and from Cathedral Catholic hurry up the hill to their respective schools. The bells began to ring and the students ran faster. Bendu smiled, turned, and went upstairs to Peace in Practice. Two new groups were set to begin the peace education and vocational training program at PIP, and Tenneh would be starting as a full-time Peer Counselor. Ever since Agnes had taken Tenneh into her home, the girl had not ceased to amaze them with her fortitude in the face of her HIV infection. Agnes was truly a saint, Bendu was sure. Bendu marveled at her friend's selflessness and her faith that God would provide everything she needed to take care of her ever-growing household.

Bendu was the first one in the office. It would be an hour before anyone else arrived. She wanted to be prepared—not just with the materials and the new schedule of activities, but also mentally. She knew her recovery would be gradual, and maybe never quite complete, but her goal was to start at a solid place with the new participants. She wanted to have a firm grip on her own feelings, even though she knew they were subject to change as she continued to grow.

Bendu sat down at her desk and took out a writing pad and a pen. She had thought about her letter all night, and had figured out what was holding her back from writing it: she had subconsciously believed that writing to the person who had caused her the most pain during the war was a negative exercise. She then decided she was going to put her own twist on the assignment, and share it with Agnes today. The writing pad was new, and still had that Standard Stationery Store scent she remembered from her own school days. It was funny how some things never changed, while others changed profoundly. She smiled to herself, and began to write.

> *Dear Benji and Granny May, I know you see every-*
> *thing I do, and I feel your spirits in those special*
> *moments when I need you most. Jonah, you opened*
> *my eyes and no one can ever take your place. I am*
> *the woman that I am because you loved me. And*
> *yes, Commander Cobra—or Moses Varney, as we*
> *call you now—this is for you too. I didn't know*
> *who I was or who I could become until you and this*
> *so-called "civil" war touched my life and changed*
> *it forever. I didn't die, and now I am stronger. I*
> *write this letter to all of you:*

It was quiet and peaceful in the office, and the words came from her heart and flowed from her pen effortlessly:

> *So much has happened in the past few months. Something about the stories from Freetown touched Calvin deeply and he returned from Sierra Leone with a softened heart. He just launched The Benjamin Lewis Jr. Memorial Scholarship Program for war-affected youth, and I pray that his old mind-set will continue to change. Siatta filed for a divorce from Terrance at the end of April and has been walking on air ever since. 'Bendu,' she explained to me, 'It's a hundred times better to be alone and free than to be trapped in a lie.' I could certainly relate to what she was feeling. Nothing casts so ominous a shadow on life as a lie, a secret, or a grudge.*

> *My daughter May is home at last. I cannot describe the joy I felt when I first laid eyes on her. She is the spitting image of Granny May. She has dark skin, beautiful almond-shaped eyes, and thick wavy hair that she refuses to straighten. 'Mama (she calls me), I don't know why the big girls at the camp put relaxers or caustic soda in their hair. It burns them, it takes all their food money, and then they go and sew false hair on top of it! Why do they do it Mama, when God gave us such beautiful hair?' I love the way she talks with a slight Ghanaian accent, and sometimes I can only smile at the questions she asks. She is so intense, and to say 'I love her so much' doesn't even begin to express how deeply I feel for her. At ten she*

is a little bit shorter and skinnier than she should be, but she's certainly eating enough now to make up for lost time. During our first few weeks together I was fully expecting some anger and resentment to surface, and constantly looked for it. I still look, but there is none. All I see in her is happiness, a childlike wonder at the new things she's learning and experiencing, and, surprisingly, a strong sense of entitlement. We are her family and she knows this is where she belongs. Her Grandma Eva spoils her rotten, and her Grandpa Ben came around the minute he saw his mother's face in hers. I've asked Calvin to be her godfather, and he deserves an Oscar or the Étalon de Yennenga for the way he is playing the role. He drives her to and from Confirmation Class every Saturday and so I continue to see him regularly. The other day May came to me and said 'Mama, can I not take the god from in his name and just call him father?' This time her question brought tears to my eyes as well as a smile to my face.

We are all still worried about the fighting in the interior, but there are signs of hope: the State of Emergency was recently lifted, and the International Contact Group on Liberia has been created to look into ways to end this civil conflict once and for all. After her experience with the Gardnersville incident, Siatta instantly became more sensitive to those of us who are used to such trauma. Her new attitude makes me think of that day in front of the American Embassy when the women cried. Even those who had not been in Liberia during the war were moved—not just to tears, but to understanding. Or at least to the understanding that they would never fully understand. Along with everyone else, I wept that day for my cousin Orlando who was captured and taken away to an unknown fate. I wept for the abandoned children who starved to death or were taken to serve as child soldiers. I cried for the helpless old people who had nurtured us and raised us, only to have us leave them to die alone. Finally, I cried for my own sins—for the terrible things I did, and for the countless times that I did nothing to help someone else.

So far, all our petitions and peace marches to the representatives of the international community have been met with a mixture of encouragement, wariness, and inaction. Some accuse us of being government-sponsored and anti-sanctions, but we are simply concerned daughters of this country and all we are asking for is peace. I'm so afraid that the international community will refuse to send the peacekeepers we have asked for until thousands more have died or been displaced. What more do we have to do? Place the bodies at their doorsteps?

I often wonder what will happen to us as a society if we never get the justice or the closure that we deserve. I have made a commitment to work toward helping us get that justice and that closure, no matter how long it takes. Peace will not come to us unless we work for it. Our efforts must be focused and our cries simply must be heard. A Truth and

Reconciliation Commission worked for South Africa,
genocide trials are still going on in Rwanda, and a
war-crimes tribunal has been approved for Sierra
Leone. What will become of us as a society if known
criminals and murderers are allowed to walk the
streets of Monrovia with no accountability for their
actions? Can we ever be at peace while the unre-
deemed and unrepentant walk among us? What
does it say about us when we allow known murderers
to hold some of the highest political offices? What
are we teaching our children?

Bendu stopped writing for a minute and looked at the photographs on her desk:

The photo of her with Jonah had been joined by photos
of young Benji laughing at something, May grinning for her
first formal portrait, and May with her old teddy bear in its
now tattered and faded blue and yellow dress—the same
one that had welcomed her to the world. There was Calvin
with a mischievous twinkle in his eye, the Lewis women all
together—Bendu, Siatta, and their mother Eva—and a lovely
candid shot of the Lewis men: her father Ben and her grand-
father Sam in their younger days, deep in conversation. Bendu
rearranged one of the frames and continued to write:

Choosing to let go was one of the hardest things I
ever did, but it has also been one of the greatest. I lost
a burden, and found a purpose far beyond myself. I
have also finally been able to accept the forgiveness
that Cousin Rebecca has so graciously offered me
all these years. And I managed—at last—to find
a safe place between remembering and forgetting.

It is a place called transformation. I can take what happened, and make something good come out of it. Change through positive action. No one knows what our future holds, but we all know that we hold our future in our hands. We often say our children are the future, but as long as we're alive and there is a tomorrow we too are the future, and we hold our destiny in our hands.

In the search for May, I tried looking up Orlando, but there was no trace of him. As Agnes says, some answers will have to wait until the afterlife. We did, however, hear something of Samson. I don't know how true it is, but "they say" he is alive and well in Danané, Côte d'Ivoire. They say he's singing now, and that everyone knows him as 'The Liberian Alpha Blondy' because of his dreadlocks and his songs for peace. In a way he was a victim, I suppose, like all of us. Or, more accurately, a survivor. If what they say is true—if Samson has redeemed himself—there is hope for everyone.

The road to redemption is a long one, with many paths branching off along the way. We may get off anywhere we want, but I'm going to keep on searching for the end of it. Peace will be my reward.

Yours Truly,
Bendu Lewis
September, 2002

Author's note: In August 2003, President Charles Taylor went into exile and the Comprehensive Peace Agreement (CPA) was signed in Accra, Ghana, bringing an end to 14 years of conflict in Liberia. As part of the agreement, a transitional government was formed, and provisions were made for a national Truth and Reconciliation Commission (TRC) to be established. Liberia's TRC was inaugurated by newly-elected President Ellen Johnson Sirleaf in early 2006. The mandate of the nine-member Commission is to investigate human rights violations and other abuses committed in Liberia between 1979 and October 2003. Their goal is to review what happened and determine the root causes of the conflict; make recommendations to the government for amnesty, prosecution, and reparations; and, hopefully, inspire reconciliation between individuals and between communities. Thousands of Liberians both at home and in the diaspora have given statements to the TRC, and public hearings began in January 2008. Victims and perpetrators—all survivors—are reaching into the bottom of their souls and telling their stories.

Acknowledgments

⁓

This story was inspired by the lives of many men, women, children, and former fighters who shared with me their experiences of the Liberian civil conflict. Without their true stories, I could not have created this work of fiction.

Several documents were very useful to me during my research—most notably the Peacebuilding and Trauma Counseling Workshop Manual created by the American Refugee Committee (Liberia, 2000), the work of peacebuilder Dr. Louise Diamond, and reports by Amnesty International and Human Rights Watch. Materials from the International Committee of the Red Cross, and an informative meeting with ICRC Tracing Assistant Albert D. Jamah, also proved invaluable.

Many individuals read excerpts and early drafts of *Redemption Road* and encouraged me along the way. I am grateful to all of them for their insights, and for their faith in this novel. In particular, special thanks to Doeba Bropleh,

Robtel Neajai Pailey, Angela M. Peabody, Lydia Sandimanie Nimley, Nazir and Deepa Ahmad, Ethan and Jude Landis, Annaird Naxela, Senator John A. Ballout, Jr., Sage Kalmus, Tehtee Sherman, Dena Singleton, Michael Weah, Kona Khasu, and the Liberia Association of Writers. I would also like to thank my colleagues from the BBC World Service Trust's "Communicating Justice" project.

I wrote this novel in three countries. For helping to take care of my family and making it possible for me to write in peace, I thank Mama Bernadette Ilunga in the DR Congo, Iqlal Zakaria in the Sudan, and Ma Edith Davies and J. T. James in Liberia. I'd also like to thank my entire family, especially my husband Shaun Skelton and our sons Keyan and Tyne, for their love and support.

Most of all, thank you to my father, Emanuel L. Shaw II, who amazes me with his knowledge and wisdom, and inspires me with his life; and to my mothers Marcia Shaw and Isabella Duncan for their friendship and encouragement.

An Invitation from the Publisher

Are you suffering the consequences of a recent civil war or violent conflict? Are you still in need of healing? Do you have a war secret or a grudge you don't want to carry any more? Maybe you simply want to tell your story. Or perhaps you still need to express your anger.

Cotton Tree Press invites you to follow in the footsteps of Tenneh and Bendu. Write a letter, and submit it for possible publication in our forthcoming anthology, *Peace in Practice: Letters from a Place of Sorrow and Hope*.

This invitation is open to readers of all nationalities, and all writing skill levels are welcome. We will also welcome "as told to" stories, so those who are literate can help the unlettered participate in this healing project too. Like the characters in *Redemption Road*, please write your letter to the person or persons you need to forgive or confront, or to whom you need to talk.

Send your letter to anthology@CottonTreePress.com. Please include your full contact information, but let us know if you want to remain anonymous, and, if your letter is selected, we will create a fictional name for you.

For general inquiries, write to info@CottonTreePress.com, or visit our website at www.CottonTreePress.com. To order additional copies of *Redemption Road*, visit our website, your local bookstore, or your favorite online bookseller.